The Meaning of

By Lee Rimmington

Copyright © 2015 Lee Rimmington

This version of the text copyright © 2018 Lee Rimmington

The right of Lee Rimmington to be identified as the author of the work has been asserted by him in accordance with the Copyright, Design and Patents act of 1988

Apart from any use permitted under UK copyright law, this publication may only be reproduced, stored or transmitted, in any form, or by any means, with prior permission, or in the case of reprographic production, in accordance with the terms and licences issued by the Copyright Licence Agency

All characters in this publication are fictitious and any resemblance to real persons, living or dead, is purely coincidental

Monster Series

1 – The Meaning of Monster

2 – Here be Humans

3 – Do not fight Monsters

4 – Human Nature

5 – The Spirit in the Forest

6 – Only Human

Dedicated to Caroline Hawkins

For giving me a kick up my backside every time I wanted to quit

Cover created by Kimberley Butterfield

Chapter 1

It was an odd day to say for sure. A flash of light, a sound so sharp that he thought his head would split in two, the taste of pineapple and pain he could not even describe. Then a jolt, a sudden shock the kind you get when you fall out of bed. Samuel later awoke in a wood. He lay on the ground staring at the sky. The pain and disorientation passed, and the world around began to come into focus. The first thing that struck him was the warmth of the sun and the lush green leaves that lay directly above him. All this told him it was most likely summer. This was indeed strange as it had been the middle of winter just a few seconds ago.

He rolled over onto his front stuck his arms out in front of him and lifted himself up off the ground. The sensation of slightly moist grass and soil greeted his palms. Samuel put himself on his feet and stood up, he wobbled for a bit as his balance came back to him. He looked around him and saw trees lots of trees. This was slightly unusual for his bedroom.

Samuel did not start with the usual response for this situation panicking, running around like a headless chicken, he had never understood the point of that, so he decided to take stock. He still had his arms, five fingers on each hand, his right ring finger was bent at an odd angle, but that was normal. Samuel had his long dancer's legs, his eyes, nose, mouth and ears. He was still clothed which was good, for some reason the thought of being somewhere strange and in his birthday suit was immensely worse.

As Samuel looked at them he saw he was wearing his favourite polo shirt a single dull red colour and old like most of his things and a black hoodie, he had a thing for black. He checked his trouser pockets, they were old but well looked after, he found in his ancient, battered, black leather wallet £20 in cash in one of the sleeves. His driver's licence with its awful picture and his phone and on his feet some trainers, black with red trim on its tongue, somewhat out of place as they were new, bought just two weeks ago. Everything was as it had been before the incident.

The next thing Samuel did was check himself for any signs of injury. Samuel felt no pain, but that was no guarantee of good health. He looked for bleeding but found none, scars and bruises, but once again he could not see any no matter where he looked. After a frantic bout of poking and prodding in every nook and cranny he could find, he gave himself the cleanest bill of health he could.

He may have been acting rationally, but in truth, he was terrified. He began to rub his wonky ring finger; he did this whenever he was nervous. Samuel looked at the wood, and he was astonished at how beautiful it was, like something out of a fairy tale, lush trees, a cooling breeze, soft grass underfoot, the sunlight trickled through the canopy onto his pasty face. A gentle smell perforated the air, a mix of honeysuckle and sugar; all this made him feel at ease.

Samuel needed a plan of some kind, he had to survive here long enough to get home, and for that, he knew what he had to find, Samuel had seen enough survival shows, he needed water. He chose a direction that felt like downhill and began to walk at a slow and steady pace "no need to rush" Samuel whispered to himself, after all, there was no way of knowing what might be up ahead.

As he trudged onward, he began to think about what had happened. Samuel had been sitting in his room playing video games and then he was here. Samuel was quite intelligent, so he tried putting his brain to the task of figuring out what had happened but all he could think of was that he, someone or something had moved him here, how or why was a different question but they could not be answered just yet. "There was no point worrying," Samuel told himself, but that was a lot easier said than done.

Samuel walked in this beautiful forest, it was almost as though it were a dream, the trees reached high into the air, there were oak, beech, chestnut trees and many others he did not know the names of. The shafts of sunlight that pierced the canopy illuminated the ground to reveal gorgeous flowers that surrounded almost every trunk. The grass that grew in between them was a deep shade of green and looked so healthy and vibrant. It was all wrong, he did not know why he couldn't think of any reason why it should, but the forest made him feel uneasy. He tried to push it out of his mind.

He walked on for an unknown amount of time, he had turned his phone off to save the battery in case Samuel really needed it at some point in the future so he could not check the time and besides Samuel could not get a signal here anyway.

It was then he heard the gentle rushing of running water. He put aside his postulating and hypothesising, threw caution to the wind and ran towards the sound until he reached a crisp, clear, somewhat small, stream.

He put his hands in the water it caressed him gently with a deep chill, Samuel brought some towards his face gave it a quick sniff, it smelled pure, and he took a refreshing sip. It tasted terrific; like something out of a dream. It was sweet, and in that instant, he immediately felt better. Samuel had done something, he had found a water source, and he had faced a life-threatening challenge and overcome it. Suddenly a great sense of pride washed over him.

He took this opportunity to get a look at himself. He gazed into the stream and saw his reflection looking directly back at him. He had short brown hair, brown eyes, in fact, Samuel had often used that word to describe himself. "Brown: a dull, boring colour, that of mud and bodily excretions" Samuel mused to himself. His nose was normal not too big or too small, and it was the same story with his mouth. Samuel's chin was also covered with a small amount of stubble not too strange for a twenty-year-old. His face also had several acne scars. The good news was that he did not see any additional scars or injuries as far as he could tell he was not hurt.

Samuel took a deep breath and sat down. He still needed two more things food and shelter. It was warm and sunny so he could go a while without both. After some careful thought, he decided to follow the river downstream, people tended to congregate around water sources, and if there was anybody around here, he could defiantly use their help.

He got up, and just as he was about to get moving, he took another look at the stream, and again the same feeling of unease washed over him. This stream was beautiful just like the forest he was surrounded by. It was around two meters wide, the water was crystal clear, and Samuel could see the bottom, it was covered in small beautifully rounded pebbles while on the surface pond skaters darted around, but it too was wrong. Samuel did not have the luxury of worrying about it right now and once again pushed the feeling out of his mind.

Samuel walked downstream and once more the questions started to pop up again, what could have done this? Why did it happen? Where was he? He came up with a million reasons... superpowers, an act of God, an experiment gone wrong or some grand cosmic joke but each theory was as ridiculous as the last. However, the fact still remained he had been transported to another location apparently instantly. This carried on for a while, and the forest continued to stretch out before him the light was slightly brighter near the stream, and he looked up. The sky appeared before him and at last, he saw something that was comforting. It at least was the same as it had always been, still blue with white clouds and there, some birds flying swiftly through the air.

The sun climbed higher in the sky and then began to sink. Samuel was becoming tired now, he must have walked for over five hours his feet ached he was sweating quite profusely. He was exhausted, and hunger was setting in. He sat himself down underneath a nearby chestnut tree facing the stream. He felt a crunch, he had crushed some flowers with his backside, a small pang of guilt filled Samuel, the flowers were indeed beautiful, but it was little compared to the cocktail of other emotions he felt. Samuel looked above the treetops and saw the glow of the setting sun. The weak orange light made his eyes heavy, as his lids began to close he continued to stare at the stream and forest and the feeling returned, that sense of otherworldliness that filled his heart with dread. His last thoughts before slumber took him were simple "this was going to be a rough night."

Darkness, Samuel could not see he grasped around for anything he could until his hands reached the cold stone. Samuel followed it around until he came to a large crack in the wall, he memorised every bit of it he could and used it as a point of reference. Samuel continued sluggishly for around twenty seconds when he came to the same crack as before. Suddenly Samuel realised where he was, in a pit. Samuel looked up and saw the sun, its radiance was inviting, he tried to climb out, but the stone walls were insurmountable even the crack provided no purchase. He screamed, hoping someone would notice, but not sound left his lips deep panic began to fill his heart. The pit seemed to be getting deeper, and it was sapping his strength. Samuel fell to his knees as the darkness embraced him dragging him deeper and deeper. He looked up once more; the light from the sun was growing fainter. Samuel made one last attempted to call for help, but the second he opened his mouth the blackness flooded in.

Samuel's eyes snapped open the bright light of the morning sun greeted him, he was motionless as his brain tried to sort out what was real and what was not until he finally realised. "A nightmare, that's all it has been" Samuel muttered to himself for reassurance as he gently rubbed his finger. He sat there for about five minutes listening to the gentle babbling of the stream, the rustle of the wind in the leaves and the soft chirping of birds. He felt damp, for one embarrassing second he thought he had wet himself, then noticing that the grass was covered with dew. Samuel dragged himself up and took a few steps towards the stream, knelt down on its bank and plunged his head in. He took gulp after gulp of the sweet water then raised his head out. The chill of the water revitalising him.

As he let the rays of light warm his body, Samuel began to reconsider his options. He had travelled for a day and found no trace of anyone. He looked at the stream and saw dragonflies dancing above the water's surface; some were engaged in dogfights as though they were old warplanes with their gossamer wing sparkling in the light. Samuel felt a pang of envy for the small insects, they did not have to worry about arriving in a strange place, all they cared about was eating and mating.

Samuel took a deep breath in through his nose and let out a loud sigh. He could not come up with a better idea than the one he had yesterday. He lifted himself up and once more continued downstream.

Several hours passed, the sun was high in the sky, and the heat from its rays was making him sweat. The stream was getting wider, and reeds began to protrude from the water's surface and every now and then he saw the outline of small fish, what kind he did not know, Samuel considered attempting to catch them for food, his hunger was becoming more rampant by the hour. However he did not settle on it, the payoff would be little compared to the amount of effort he would have to put in.

Further along his trek, something caught Samuel's eye. He turned his head sharply and gazed across to the other bank. As he scanned the tree line, he saw a rock formation. There was a set of boulders just out of sight, obscured by the tree trunks, but from what he could make out they had been arranged, placed there deliberately, this was his first sign of people since he got here.

Samuel decided to investigate. He untied his shoelaces, took off his trainers and socks, picked them both up with his left hand and began to ford the stream. It was only about four meters wide, but it was going to be difficult. The water that had been so cool and refreshing in his mouth now stung his feet and legs while the pebbles, which lined the bottom, though smoothed by the stream's flow dug into the soles of his feet.

As he reached the other side, his feet finally felt the release of the soft grass. Samuel walked towards the stones. He arrived at a small clearing there were three rocks all arranged symmetrically in a triangle. The shaft of light the rolled form the canopy bathed it in a light that gave the stones a heavenly glow. The rocks, made out of granite, had indeed been set there, they were all roughly the same height as Samuel, not only that they had been carved into specific shapes, the one nearest to him was circular, with a diamond shape in the centre. The second was a cube with many spherical nodules covering it and in the centre of this stone was also a symbol, two triangles placed side by side. The third was a pyramid with three sides and had a symbol in the centre, five circles one on top of the other. All three stones appeared new, carved recently, as no apparent weathering could be found.

Samuel walked to the centre of the triangle and noticed that the three stones all had their emblems facing inward. This was a mystery, good Samuel liked mysteries. They could possibly be a warning or border maker, it was undoubtedly removed from any type of village or town, but if that were the case the symbols on them would be facing outward not inward. It could be a religious site, it certainly must have taken a lot of effort to move these stones here as well as much dedication to carve them into their respective shapes. It seemed, however, to be underused, almost forgotten, mosses and lichen grew on every one of them. Samuel could not imagine that anyone would treat a holy site with such neglect. Most likely, he surmised, this was a monument placed there to commemorate such a great achievement or event.

Walking back towards the stone with the diamond patterned, Samuel knelt down and placed his hand upon the stone, it was surprisingly warm, heated by the sun, and ran his fingers upon its surface. The stone was wonderfully smooth. His fingers came to the symbol engraved upon it, and he tried to make sense of it, the diamond had to mean something, but no matter how hard he worked nothing came to him. Samuel believed that he needed more information if he was going to answer this question.

Samuel stood back up and began to search the stones and the area around them for any sign of activity. He checked for footprints, out of place rocks and broken twigs but it was futile, he was no scout, and he found nothing. If this was a monument, nobody visited it or at least not recently. "Damn," Samuel said in a low, annoyed tone. If anyone did live around here, he had no idea where.

Samuel faced the diamond stone and walked towards it once more. Stood in front of it for a few seconds and then walked past it back towards the stream. This encounter had been both uplifting and disheartening.

As he came back to the stream he turned facing downstream once more "this was getting tedious" he thought to himself, Samuel placed his shoes and socks back on his feet, and continued his march to find someone, anyone who could help him, tell him what had happened and especially where he was.

Slowly the worries began to sink in what if he never got home? What if he died here alone, with no one around? His body going putrid in the sun, had anyone noticed that he was gone? Did anyone even care? The worry and despair he began to feel were crippling him, Samuel's chest was tight, he felt sick, and he started to panic. Samuel rubbed his ring finger vigorously and told himself to be calm and he should be rational in this situation after all this kind of thinking would only lead to his death. However, this line of thought was not making him feel better. It was then he heard the gentle sound of high-pitched laughter.

The sensation of that sound hitting his ears filled his heart with elation he had never known. All the tormenting emotions that had clouded his senses evaporated. The sound was coming from deeper in the forest, from the other side of the river. Samuel crossed the river again, paying little attention to the stones that had once plagued him so, and began to walk hurriedly but cautiously towards it, he could not be sure that they were friendly after all. As he came closer, the laughter became more evident, and it began to sound more and more like that of children. This was good. Children tended to be less dangerous than adults. Up ahead he could see a large boulder, and whoever these people were, they were behind it. Cautiously he peered around it.

The children were playing. At least he thought they were children. One, a boy about the age of seven, had a human appearance until you came to look at his legs they appeared to be covered in armour like that of a beetle, he had compound eyes and antenna on his head. His arms also shared the same insectoid motif. The second one, a girl around ten, was normal down to her hips which then became a snake's tail. The final one was also a girl, again about seven, was covered in white wool with horns on her head and cloven hooves for feet.

Samuel retreated behind the boulder and thought "riiiiight." An insect boy, a Lamia and a sheep child; what was this, a fantasy RPG? He peered back to get a better look all the while rubbing his finger. First he inspected the boy, the child had short black hairstyles similarly to Samuels except it looked like an amateur had cut it. The boy also had iridescent eyes like the rainbows petrol made in water. His arms and legs covered in black chitin that shined beautifully in the sun the leg armour came up as high as his calf. The boy's antenna also twitched at regular intervals. The Lamia had golden hair it was very long coming all the way down to her hips, the scales on her tail were the same colour as her hair, and her eyes were orange with slit pupils like a cat. The sheep girl had yellow horns on her head; the wool was not universal in coverage it congregated around her forearms, lower legs and chest.

Samuel also noted that the hair on her head was also made of the same wool that was on the rest of her body, but it came down to her shoulders and appeared to have been styled slightly there were also red ribbons strewed throughout.

The clothes they were wearing were exceptionally intriguing. They were simple like the tunics that peasants used to wear in the dark ages, but the colours were anything but. The insect boy's tunic was purple. The Lamia wore an unusually long tunic; a blue article with red pattered about it shaped like diamonds. The sheep girl did not wear a top, but she did wear a skirt, purple like the boys but a lighter shade. None of them wore shoes, for the Lamia, this was not unsurprising, but Samuel guessed the chitin and hooves provided ample protection from stones and other potential hazards.

The game they were playing intrigued him, what were they playing? The two girls had sticks in their hands as they brandished them at the boy, but it did not seem like they were bullying him, as he smiled broadly. He said something but what Samuel could not tell what, they were not speaking English or any language he had ever heard before, he stood on a nearby rock clutching a far longer stick and laughed. The sheep girl spoke next, again in the same language, the look on her face; he had seen it many times in films when heroes spoke to the villain.

The boy said something else and gestured his hand to the two girls and then closed his fist tightly and roared, at least he tried to, but it was more of a squeak. Then it clicked, what they were playing it was a game Samuel had often enjoyed when he was a boy. The girls were knights', or something similar, protecting their friends and families, the boy was a monster, dragon, dark lord or some such, attempting to destroy them. Samuel continued to stare and giggled slightly this greatly eased his mind, where ever he was it still had children no matter how they looked and if they were happy it meant that things could not be so bad around here. The Lamia child must have heard Samuel's faint laughing because she turned around to face him.

She looked at him for just moment and then spoke in that strange language, and the other two froze and looked at Samuel as well. The children and Samuel stared at one another for what seemed like an age. The boy spoke to the two girls, the sheep girl responded, then the Lamia waved her had at the other two and then talked to Samuel, and beckoned him to come forward. Samuel thought about it as she continued to call him, though the other two were far less keen than her. Samuel needed food and shelter and these kids there his best bet. After all, they seemed pleasant, and he did not believe in judging a book by its cover. He sighed and took a step out from behind the rock.

The three children stared at him, their eyes widened and their faces contorted into a visage of pure terror, and that is when the screaming started.

Chapter 2

That sound, that ungodly sound. The three children screamed at the top of their lungs as the sound tore through Samuel's eardrums. When the children finally ran out of breath the boy jumped straight for the Lamia and clung to her. they stared at Samuel the fear no less prevalent on the faces. "What's the matter" Samuel spoke as softly as he could.

These kids were terrified of him, and he did not know why. He took a step forward, in hindsight, not the best move, and the children almost jumped backwards. The sheep girl began to cry, and the little Lamia pointed her stick straight at Samuel and spoke to him in a threatening tone, but she could not mask the fear. The boy said something else, fear emanating from every word. Samuel stared at the stick and as gently as he could and said "I am not going to hurt you", but all that succeeded in doing was making them take another step back, although the Lamia did more of a wriggle. Samuel outstretched his arm and opened his hand taking another step towards them. That was the last straw, they turned around at a fantastic speed and darted off into the forest.

Samuel was left standing there with a look of sheer confusion on his face. Nothing, nothing he had experienced up until that point in his entire life could have prepared him for that. His knees let out, and Samuel slumped to the floor his outstretched arm hit the floor palm facing up. Tears began to well up in his eyes; the way they had looked at him was awful as though he was not a person, just a dangerous animal. "Why had they done that?" Samuel asked himself, his voice breaking slightly as he tried to stop himself from crying.

He looked at the section of forest the children had darted off to. They had dropped their sticks. Samuel picked himself up, walking towards where the children had been standing and grabbed one the makeshift swords. Despair started to take hold of him once more but also guilt, he had ruined their game, and Samuel turned around and walked back towards the boulder, he did not know why he did this. He stood there staring at the rock, and all of his thoughts just stopped all expect [except] the desire to rub his ring finger.

His mind flashed back to the time when he was around six or seven. He had been out with his parents on his bike, going down a particularly steep and rocky hill, when he lost control of his ride and tumbled head over heels on the ground. When he came to he was in the hospital, Samuel had escaped the worst of it, in fact, the doctors had been astonished that all he had broken was a single finger. That event had left his finger permanently disfigured, and he rubbed it every time he was sad or nervous.

How much time had passed he did not know. Samuel heard rustling behind him; this snapped him back to the real world. A woman appeared from behind the trees. She was a sheep woman, and she looked remarkably similar to the young sheep girl, Samuel assumed she must be her mother. The wool that covered her body was the same colour as the little girls, but her horns were black. The hair on her head was cut short, and she had ribbons in her hair as well; spring green in colour. She wore a skirt, a shade of bright yellow, that came down to her knees. Something struck Samuel almost instantly, she was gorgeous she really was in every conceivable way, horns, hooves and all and it made Samuel uneasy. There was not a single defect or flaw it was as though a sculptor had carved her out of marble.

The woman was talking to the children she had a warm smile on her face. Samuel had seen that smile many times when he was a child and had gone to his mum about the monster that he thought that had lived under his bed. The woman spoke once more; she also used the same language as the children and gave a small chuckle. When she turned to face Samuel she froze, and the smile evaporated, and the same look of horror covered her face. Samuel hated that look. She raised her arms to stop the children from going any further.

Samuel had a good idea about what had happened. The children had run home to tell their parents about the horrible thing they had seen in the woods. The parents naturally did not believe them, nothing like what the kids had seen could possibly exist, so one of them agreed to go to the spot they had seen it, to prove that there was nothing to worry about, it was just their overactive imaginations. Only this time the nightmare was real.

The three children peered around from behind a tree, the same look of terror on their faces as before, the sheep girl glanced at her mother and back to Samuel and said something, and Samuel thought that just for a second he saw a small look of smug satisfaction on her face; at having been proven right.

The woman yelled at the children, Samuel guessed she had told them to run as the second she finished her sentence the children bolted back the way they came. Samuel had been staring intently, the entire time partly out of curiosity, partly in fear by mostly out of frustration. He was frustrated, he was angry he was sick and tired of people being fearful of him the moment they saw.

Samuel turned his entire body around to face the woman at an impressive speed, so fast, in fact, the woman almost jumped out of her skin. "Why are you so afraid of me" Samuel yelled. The woman took a step back "I have done nothing to you, and yet you all look at me like that" a slight pause that seemed like an eternity Samuel's voice lowered slightly "like I am a monster." The woman, of course, did not understand a word of it but even if she had it would probably have made little difference the venom in Samuel's voice was undeniable.

The woman turned and charged off in a different direction from the one the children had, most likely in an attempt to draw attention to her and make him give chase like a mother bird distracting a predator. Samuel however still had enough common sense to stay where he was, chasing them would only make their opinion of him even worse, although he was not entirely sure if that was possible at this point. As he stood there shifting his gaze from where the woman had left to the spot where the children had, a realisation dawned on Samuel. When either the children returned home without the woman or the woman returned without the children, they would automatically assume the worst and then blame Samuel.

Samuel's imagination began to run wild with imaginings of what would happen if the rest of these people would do to him if they got their hands on him. They would almost certainly kill him, regardless of his innocence, because as much as he could tell from their reactions of the four he had met, they held him in extremely low regard, barely considering him to be a person.

For just an instant a thought flashed across his mind "let them." Samuel was tired, he was hungry; he was an emotional wreck, and if this was what his life was going to be from now on, being hunted down like an animal, never having a moment of peace, it might as well come to an end. Then another thought surfaced "NO!" He was not going to die like this being ripped to shreds for some imagined grievances by some bigoted degenerates. "He would live" no matter what this world threw at him and with renewed vigour and determination Samuel set off into the forest.

Samuel walked at an impressive pace, deciding to run only when it was necessary, attempting to put as much distance between him and whoever might follow.

Samuel did not know where he was going at this point he only wanted to get away. Samuel, of course, could not be sure that they would try to harm him, nothing that had happened could confirm that, but he was not acting or thinking entirely rationally at the moment. He was beginning to assume the worst about everything.

At this very moment, he was angry "how dare they treat me like that" Samuel grumbled to himself "didn't anyone teach them manners." Then a new question raced across his mind "why had they acted like that?" All it had taken was one look at Samuel, and the children screamed while the woman had attempted to protect them. Samuel would have expected that response if they had encountered a bear. "Had they had a terrible encounter with a human before?"

"Human before," said Samuel with a humourless chuckle "listen to me!" Acting as though all this was entirely natural, Samuel was feeling extremely depressed. Samuel walked off in a kind of trance as all of his new information collided inside is mind. He was abruptly snapped out of it when he heard something out in the distance, his first thought was "they've found me" but the sound was not that of people talking, he stopped and listened. It was a low and booming, and it was coming clearer and clearer. It was barking, they had dogs. Samuel had not counted on this, if dogs were tracking him it did not matter where he hid, his sent [scent] would give him away, Samuel started moving again but quickened his pace, he had to locate somewhere the dogs or their owners could not find him.

Their braying was getting louder, and Samuel's pace quickened, he was jogging now, the thud of each of his footsteps shook his body. Already his breath was becoming rapid, and sweat began to cover his brow. Then it struck his ears, in between the barks he heard the unmistakable voices of people, they had almost found him, and now he ran.

Samuel galloped through the wood as fast as he could, fear gripping him tightly. He tried his best to remember everything his P.E teacher had told him to breathe through his nose out through the mouth, he wished he had listed [listened] more instead of drawing insulting pictures of the teacher in the long jump pit. Samuel turned his head ever so slightly to see behind him and caught a glimpse of something behind him, it was big, it was hairy, and it darted rapidly through the trees, Samuel sprinted as hard as he could.

He charged through the forest, the noise behind him a reminder of what would happen if he was caught. Up ahead he could see a fallen tree, half his height, he did not dare slow down, so he leapt. If Samuel could have could have seen himself in action he would have been impressed, his form was perfect, and the height he had cleared was impressive, possibly even Olympic quality, but at the moment he was focused on only one thing.

As he ran further and further the noise of his pursuers was getting fainter. Samuel was suspicious, but his lungs were burning, his legs ached, and the adrenaline pumping through his body was making his teeth chatter. He slowed down and took a much-needed breather behind a tree. As Samuel stood there panting between his legs, hoping that all this was just another nightmare until something in the corner of his eye caught his attention. He turned right to face it.

They had led him into a trap. "Clever bitch!" Samuel yelled he was face to face with a dog, although it looked more like a wolf. It was huge with jet black fur, its obsidian eyes glared at him all the while it snarled at him bearing its yellow teeth. Samuel tried to think of the best course of action but before he could the dog leapt.

As the weight of the animal crashed down on top of Samuel, he let out a brief grunt. The beast was massive, its legs pushed into Samuel's chest making it difficult to breathe. Samuel's left hand went up, and he grabbed the dog's throat. The dog continued to the bite and gnash at him regardless, its breath smelled horrible as though it had only eaten rotten meat its entire life. Samuel pulled his head back as far as he could to prevent the animal from getting at his neck.

His arm was beginning to tire, and every second the dog came closer and closer. Samuel attempted to find something to strike the dog with. As Samuel grasped around, he realised he was still holding the stick he had picked up, the one the children had been playing with. Samuel struck the side of the dog's head. The stick broke on its skull, but the animal did not seem to notice, it paused for about half a second, and continued to attack. Samuel glanced at the pretend sword. It had broken into a sharp point. He rotated the stub around in his hand and held it like a steak. With all his might Samuel rammed it into the dogs face.

Warm fluid rushed over his hand, and the dog yelped; it had felt that one. The dog jumped off Samuel forcing out what was left of the air in his lungs. He crawled to his feet, looked back at the animal that had almost killed him, and noticed that the steak had gone straight into the creature's eye socket. The animal pawed at it attempting to remove the foreign body, but it was undoubtedly making it worse. Samuel's modern sensibilities told him he should feel sorry for it, but he didn't. Samuel panted as the shock wore off and once again a sense of accomplishment came over him. The next thing he knew he was falling to the ground.

He felt a great force charge into his back. He crashed face down onto the ground then a few seconds later Samuel felt a sharp aching pain in his side. Samuel mustered all of his strength and rolled over on his back.

Compound eyes greeted his. It was another insect person, a man this time. His eyes too were iridescent, their gaze pierced Samuel, and there on his face a look of both horror and rage. He bore his teeth at Samuel a full set of razor-sharp canines. He spoke, Samuel could not tell what it was but from the tone, volume and the situation he guessed it was "DIE!"

The man reached for Samuel's throat, his arms covered in sapphire blue chitin, and they clamped firmly around his neck. Samuel gasped for air, his legs kicked wildly attempting to get free, and his lungs began to strain in the attempt to draw in oxygen. Samuel's vision was becoming blurred; if he did not do something quickly, he would pass out. He did the only thing he could. Samuel clenched his hand into a fist and brought it, with all the force he could muster, squarely onto his assailant's face. It was at this moment Samuel learned a valuable lesson; punching someone... really hurts.

The man released his grip on his throat, it was not gentle however, he almost crushed Samuel's windpipe in the process, without thinking Samuel brought his leg up towards his chest and propelled it towards his attacker's face. The insect man reeled back from the impacted and the pain, clutching his face. Samuel was on all fours coughing and spluttering on the ground while his attacker just a couple of metres away rolled around in agony. Judging from the man's reaction he had either broken or dislocated his jaw.

Samuel hauled himself up and took in deep breaths in an attempt to control his breathing. Over the cries and yelps of his would be killers he heard a familiar sound, the rest of the mob was after him again. Samuel was running on fumes now, nothing keeping him going but his strength of will, the fight had taken much out of him and all Samuel could manage was a slow jog. The sounds were getting closer, he heard a twang, then felt something rush past his ear, up ahead he saw an arrow embed itself into a nearby tree. "GREAT" he yelled "they don't actually have to catch me to kill me".

In the near distance, he saw a bright light. The trees were beginning to thin. Samuel prayed they would not follow him out of the forest's borders, it was a desperate hope, but it was the only one he had. Samuel burst from the trees and saw before him saw a huge drop.

Samuel skidded to a halt. Right in front of him was a cliff, at least twenty metres high, and below that a lake. It was huge, the lake extended almost to the horizon. Samuel looked to his left and to his right, in both directions stretched miles of clear open ground no more than ten metres wide. He realised he was now left with three options. First, stand his ground and attempt to fight; Samuel knew there was no way he could manage that.

Second stay on the cliff and run in either direction a better chance than fighting but he could not run forever, and with a clear line of sight, his pursuers would almost certainly hit him with one of their arrows. The final choice was to just jump. It was not that Samuel did not know how to swim, in truth he could swim quite well, the problem was that he could not tell how deep the water was, whether he would land on solid ground just half a metre underneath, or if there were rocks underneath, and falling on those was also not an appealing option.

Samuel was not good at snap decisions and tried his best to weigh his options in the little time he had. The shouting grew louder, and Samuel rubbed his right hand's ring finger. Samuel hated heights, but he hated the idea of being ripped to pieces and eaten by dogs even more. With fear, desperation and no small amount of courage, he took the plunged.

The wind rushed all around him, while a deep sense of vertigo overcame him. He did his best to keep his legs straight as hit the water. Strange that the fall did not take as long as he thought it would. Bitterly cold water engulfed him. Samuel had however forgotten to take a breath before jumping, and as he realised this, he made a desperate attempt to reach the surface. As he breached, he took in what seemed the greatest and sweetest breath of his life.

He was alive, that was good, Samuel twisted around in the water to get his bearings and saw the cliff he had just leapt from towering above him. He swam as fast as he could towards its face. Just in time to, for the shadows of his hunters appeared on the water.

Samuel pressed himself as tight as he could against the wall; if any of them looked directly down, he was finished. He heard them talking, shouting really. Some were angry, others satisfied, and some oddly enough, were disappointed like a hunter that had just lost a prized buck. Then he felt a warm sensation around his legs.

He looked to his right and saw a slight indentation in the rock. As slowly and gently as he could, trying to prevent the creation of any ripples on the water that may alert his pursuers, inched closer to it. He slid into the crevice. Just after Samuel got in one of the shadows pointed, Samuel froze, he had slipped up at the last second, and before him, he saw a small wave radiate away from him.

The people had started talking again, Samuel wished he could understand, it might have given some motivation for their aggressive behaviour. The talking died down, Samuel assumed they believed the rippled had been caused by a fish. One of them said something else, and then the mob separated into two groups and ran off in opposite directions along the cliff front.

Samuel had not moved an inch. Five minutes later he breathed a sigh of relief. Samuel was safe for now, but his limbs were becoming heavy, the adrenaline was wearing off, and if he stayed here, he would drown. He looked behind and saw that the crevice was, in fact, a cave that extended deep into the rock.

Reluctant to swim out into open water and intrigued by the warm water flowing from the cave he proceeded further inside. It was quite cramped but not impossible to move down, and he was never worried about becoming stuck. The water came up to his collarbone with the ceiling just thirty centimetres above his head. What intrigued him was the cave itself, the walls were smooth and perfectly rectangular, without any crags or imperfections, as if somebody had carved it, more like a tunnel really.

The light from outside was fading, and it was becoming increasingly difficult to see. Touch was quickly becoming his only means of navigation. That being said Navigation was unnecessary, the tunnel was as straight as a ruler. The walls were warm to the touch, heated by the water, and the rock had a lovely texture like polished marble. Samuel knew that this was not a natural formation; someone had built it, he had learned in geography that water never flows completely straight.

He began to slow down, partly out of exhaustion, mostly because the people that had built the tunnel could be close by and they could be just as hostile as the others, it might have been his pursuers that had created it.

Samuel continued at a snail's pace until he saw a faint blue glow. Samuel submerged himself down to his mouth and gently paddled towards it. The light gently illuminated the tunnel once more, and he took another look at the rock around him. It had a dark hue, with white streaks through it, whatever this tunnel was for it was meant to be aesthetically pleasing. Then before he even realised the tunnel expanded into a colossal cavern.

It was stunning both in scale and beauty. The forest and stream had been wonders in their own right, but this was on a whole other level. The tunnel was merely an outlet for an underground lake, nowhere near as big as the one outside, it was still impressive though. Steam was coming off the surface. "It's a hot spring" Samuel whispered with much awe.

Under the water, he saw shapes moving, he panicked for a second, but it quickly subsided. They were fish, big fish, around the length of his forearm. The fish were pale in colour, which was unusual, but what was most surprising was how docile they were. They swam around him like he was just another rock.

Samuel looked around but saw no one, tired and wanting to feel solid ground underfoot. He set off for the nearest bank. The warmth of the water was seeping into his muscles making them extremely relaxed; if he stayed in here much longer, he would fall asleep. He reached the edge and hauled himself out of the water and rolled onto his back. As he looked up, he saw stars.

Stars on the roof of the cave, which could not be right. It was still daylight outside, and yet there they were, tiny twinkly lights, thousands of them on the roof. Part of him wanted to investigate further, but his stomach had other ideas. Now the danger was over it growled furiously, he had never been this hungry before in his life. Samuel rolled onto his stomach and crawled towards the water's edge.

Samuel rolled up his sleeve; his clothes were soaking wet, so it did not really make any difference, and gently placed his arm in the water with his hand open and waited for one of the fish to swim in close. He lay there patiently, soon the rest of the world became dead to him, Samuel had never been this focused in his life. Time appeared to slow down, he no longer felt the stone he was lying on or the heat of the water. Then one particularly brave or stupid fish ventured a little too close, and Samuel struck.

His hand grasped the fish as hard has it could and pulled it out of the water. The fish wriggled as hard as it could to escape but it was fruitless, Samuels grip was so tight he had crushed some of the animal's bones. As hungry as he was he did not want to make the fish suffer so he adjusted his hold to the end of its tail and brought it down hard against the stone. There was a sickening crunch as the fish's skull was crushed.

The animal was left on the floor, blood trickled from its head, and the fish gave an involuntary spasm and then stopped moving altogether. Samuel picked up the recently deceased fish, he felt a little sorry for the poor creature, He had another problem now, he had no means of starting a fire or preparing it, and so with no other options, he brought it up to his mouth. Samuel took a deep breath and bit into the animals back.

The animal's body crunched as his teeth broke the fish's ribs and spine. He pulled away a large chunk of flesh. He stuck his hands into his mouth and pulled out all of the bones he had taken away with it. He paused for just a moment and then began to chew. It was slimy, it was tough, it was surprisingly good actually, after two days with nothing to eat; Samuel was not focusing on eating a raw fish that he had killed himself but on how excellent the meat was. Its flavour was light, and it had a firm texture. Samuel took bite after bite eating almost every part of the animal, its heart, liver, but not the guts or stomach, he did not want to get infected with worms.

Samuel placed what was left of the fish to one side. His stomach now full, his eyes began to become heavy, all of the fatigue of the day was coming back to him, he lay down on his back and gazed up back towards the ceiling, back to the lights, and a familiar feeling came back to him; it was wrong. This cavern had saved his life, it was majestic, but it gave Samuel a deep sensation in the pit of his stomach. Samuel began to worry that this night would be just as bad as the last. With that, the world was lost to him, and he slept.

Chapter 3

There was no nightmare this time. In fact, Samuel could not be entirely sure he had slept at all. His eyes opened slowly, and the starry ceiling met his sight. He tried to get up but the aching pain was unimaginable, every muscle in his body had cramped during the night, and even moving a finger sent a jolt of agony down his arm. Samuel stretched his right arm, it hurt, but he could not lay there forever, he then swung his right arm over his body and pushed up to that he was on his stomach. Then placing his left arm on the floor, and attempted to lift himself onto his knees but the pain forced him back down. Determined Samuel tried again, breathing deep with every motion, and this time he succeeded.

Samuel put himself on one foot, and with one quick motion, maybe too quick, lifted himself onto his feet. "AARRGGHH" Samuel yelled as all of his muscle commanded him to get back to the floor. He ignored them and took a step forward and stumbled slightly. Samuel thought back to the other day, specifically the chase, he had never exercised so much in his life, and this pain was his body telling him to never attempted to run like an athlete without practice first.

He noticed that he was still wet. The steam rising from the pool kept the air humid and prevented his clothes from drying out. Samuel took off his shoes, socks, trousers, hoodie and shirt. he kept his underwear on, taking them off would have made him feel vulnerable, and lay them out nice and neat on a low-hanging ledge. Then he remembered his phone he darted to his trousers and pulled both it and his wallet out of the pockets. He attempted to turn it on, but nothing he did was able to do so, it had become waterlogged. "DAMN" Samuel screamed, he liked that phone, he put it to one side and then opened his wallet, his £20 note was ruined and become a blank sheet of fabric, but aside from that everything else was fine.

Samuel turned to face the pool and took in his surroundings. The first thing that became apparent was how warm it was in the cavern, the steam made the air close, even the stone he was standing on was warm. "The water must warm this entire place" Samuel mused to himself "at least I won't freeze to death when winter rolls around," he said to the humid air.

Samuel then noticed how thirsty he was and he hobbled towards the water. Kneeling down he cupped his hands and brought some of the warm liquid to his face. It was just about how he expected it to be. Warm water was never very nice, but it did the trick his thirst vanished. As he stood back up he smacked his lips, he could taste that the water was full of minerals, not surprising really for a hot spring.

As he stood there, wriggling his toes, he noticed that surrounding the pool was a series of ledges of varying height but what was strange about them was that they were all perfectly square, not a single rounded edge among them. He walked up to the nearest one to examine it, his legs protesting with each step, the stone was made out of the same material as the tunnel. The ledge came up to his knees, and with a bit of effort, he climbed on top of it.

Looking back at where he had slept he noticed that the area was utterly flat, he then looked back to the ledges. Then he saw that the entire area was arranged like a theatre, the flat area was the stage and the ledges the seats. This place did not just look like a pool, it was a pool. This entire area had been carved out of solid rock it had taken time and effort on an unimaginable scale, and it was merely a luxury, whoever built this clearly had never faced the difficulties Samuel had. For some reason, the knowledge, or more accurately the assumption, that this place was not, in fact, a natural formation made the sense of unease he had felt before vanish.

Samuel climbed up from one ledge to the next, moving was becoming easier now, to get a better view of this impressive feat of engineering. As he climbed higher and higher, Samuel was now about fifteen meters off the ground, he looked up at the lights on the ceiling. They were coming into focus, and he could have sworn that they were moving.

Another ledge presented itself before Samuel, it was taller than he was, with a slight hop he grabbed the top of the ledge. Samuel attempted to haul himself up but it was indeed a struggle, Samuel's arms strained under the effort of hauling his twelve stone frame. He let go, the edges of the ledge had begun to dig into his palms, and the rock was slightly slippery from the damp air.

Samuel, however, was undeterred. Taking a few steps back, as far away from the ledge he wanted to climb as he could, he made a quick sprint and jumped. Once more he grabbed the ledge, but this time he used his legs. His feet scrabbled against the side, it was actually rather funny watching this under toned young man scrabble up the wall in only his boxer shorts, but slowly he climbed higher.

He placed his right arm onto the top of the ledge and then swung his left leg onto it as well, and with a little bit more effort finally succeeded in dragging his entire body up.

Getting himself back on his feet he was now on the highest ledge in the cavern. Looking down he got a slight sense of vertigo. Shaking his head slightly he turned his attention to the lights. They were much clearer now, and they were indeed moving. Then Samuel observed something more, the lights were being dragged behind long, thin, almost transparent tubes. Samuel finally realised what they were...worms, thousands upon thousands of worms.

The entire ceiling was crawling with them. Glow worms, so many they illuminated the whole cavern. A slight sense of disgust washed over Samuel, but this was quickly replaced with one of wonder and awe.

Samuel drew his face closer to inspect the worms more closely. They were around fifteen centimetres long with no visible head. When they moved, their entire body contracted and then extended again. Samuel reached his hand up towards the ceiling and prodded the nearest worm. It immediately pulled itself in a thick tube of mucus, like a fat slug, and its backside began to flash like a strobe light.

A small amount of slime stuck to his finger. "Eww," Samuel said in a deliberately over the top fashion. He wiped his finger on the wall. These creatures were impressive, all of them living on barren rock, holding on no matter what life threw at them. Samuel admired the little worms for their perseverance.

Samuel looked away from his living light bulbs and back to the cavern as a whole. He saw in the distance that one ledge extended out over the pool, it was long and relatively thin "huh a diving board" said Samuel with slight indifference. "Wait a minute, how did it take me this long to notice a great chunk of rock poking out of the wall?" he said to himself in an insulting tone.

Shaking his head; in disbelief at his idiocy. He sat down, placing his head in his hands until one more point of interest caught his eye. Around fifty meters from the edge of the pool was a rectangular opening. It was another tunnel that led away from the cavern. Of course, there was a tunnel; if this place was man made it had to have an entrance. "I really am an idiot," Samuel said to himself "I honestly did not see a big, gaping hole in the wall until now."

Samuel pinched the bridge of his nose and sighed. He jumped down from the ledge and climbed down towards the opening. He slipped slightly half way down and fell on his backside. His breathing became sharp, and a sudden adrenaline spike surged through his body. If he had fallen, he would have, almost certainly, cracked his head open.

He proceeded far more steadily than he had before. He reached the bottom and walked towards the opening. He stopped along the way to check on his clothes, "still damp" he mumbled to himself. As he approached the entrance, he saw that it was around three metres in height and four metres wide. The glow from the cavern only reached approximately ten metres down its length before total darkness won out.

As he took a few steps forward, Samuel paused, judging whether or not he should step into the blackness. He was safe here, as long as he watched his steps, he had food, clean water and shelter and he had no idea what might await him, but he could not stand the thought of spending fifty years inside a cave. In the end, he decided to take the risk.

He took step after step, his bare feet slapping on the ground, leaving the gentle light of the worms behind. The air quickly became dry, but the warmth did not change, a good idea finally surfaced in his head, after the myriad of terrible ones. Samuel jogged back into the cavern, collected his clothes and carried them down the corridor.

Samuel lay them down in the corridor; the warm, dry air would get rid of the dampness much more quickly. He took a few more steps, and the darkness swallowed him. Samuel continued further along the corridor, proceeding slowly, being careful with each step in case the ground suddenly gave way. He placed his hands on the wall feeling for any kind of defect or imperfection, but he found none, its smooth rock was flawless.

After around ten minutes he saw ahead of him a faint shaft of light perforate the darkness. The weak light allowed a small flight of steps to be just barely visible. Samuel took four steps up and banged his head "Bugger" Samuel grunted rubbing his scalp.

Removing his hand from his head, a dull throb echoed throughout his skull, he placed his hands on the ceiling and ran his fingers along the seam where the light trickled through. A slight draft came through the crack. He put both of his hands on the ceiling and gave a sharp push. The ceiling moved ever so slightly. It was a slab and beyond it was the outside world. Taking two more steps up and using his legs he pushed up, the slab was heavy but not immovable. Slowly the stone was raised higher until it high enough for the light from outside to brighten up the corridor, and a gust of cool air flooded into the passage.

The air that rushed past him chilled him to the bone. It was not that the wind was unusually cold, it was just that it was very warm inside and Samuel could feel the difference; Samuel lowered the slab back down and walked back inside, rubbing his body, and realised that he was dry, so he ran back down the corridor. He eventually reached his clothes. Samuel had been right; his clothes had almost completely dried out in the parched air. He dressed and once again proceeded down the corridor.

He made his way back to the stairs and once more lifted the slab up. The air was still cold but much easier to bear. There was, however, another problem. He had become so accustomed to the darkness and dull light underground the sharp rays of the sun stung his eyes.

He snapped them shut and retreated underground. Once the pain had passed, he decided on a new strategy. He lifted up the slab slightly and then slid it along the ground. Slowly he stepped out from the underground, and he could not believe what he saw. He found himself in another cave.

All that effort just to discover another cave. However, this one was nothing like the one Samuel had slept in. This one had jagged, rough rock formations and was very shallow. This one had been forged by nature.

He took the last few steps upward and fully emerged into the outside world. He looked out of the cave and saw a slight clearing that radiated from its mouth. The orange sun hung low in the sky, it was either early morning or late evening, either way, he had slept all night.

He turned his head to look at the steps, the slab was clearly out of place, its beautiful, glistening form a stark contrast to the rough, ugly stone that surrounded it. This puzzled him slightly, after all, if he could notice something so obvious, why had no one else done so? He had found no evidence that anyone but him had ever set foot in the cavern.

Samuel chalked it up to shear bad luck on everyone else's part. Samuel was about to leave when he suddenly remembered the slab. He moved towards it and pushed it back into place, with a slight gap so that he could remove it again with little effort, and then left the cave. It needed a name.

He needed something that fitted this unnecessary addition to his home. "The extension, that certainly fits" Samuel chuckled to himself, Samuel's neighbour had had one installed when he was young the noise had bothered him immensely, and he had disliked them ever since. With that, he stepped out once again into the outside world.

The forest stretched out before him. It was gorgeous as always, the dew in the tree leaves reflected the sunlight, the leaves looked like they were made of gold, but it was still unnerving. Looking at the forest from the outside for the first time made it seem all the more malicious. However, it could just be that he knew who waited for him inside.

Samuel turned himself around, and he took in the sight of a vast rock formation that stretched many metres into the air. The cave was set in it. The stone looked as though they were the remains of a once mighty mountain, eroded after countless millennia. It all seemed rather sombre and out of place in the middle of the forest.

Samuel decided to do some exploring, keeping the small mountain to his left, he set off. Samuel was not yet confident enough to enter the forest again, and he concluded that he would first become more familiar with the land before venturing out under its canopy once more.

He ran his left hand along the stone, not for any particular reason he just felt like it. The rough texture of the rock began to make his fingers feel numb after a while. Each step brought him further away from his new home, and it made him slightly nervous.

The sun was climbing higher in the sky, so it was indeed morning after all, and the day steadily became warmer. Samuel was once again reminded of home it had been December only three days ago so why was it summer. This place was strange indeed.

His thoughts began to drift to the previous day. Samuel tried to make sense of all that had happened. First, the children had seen his face, this itself had not frightened them, it was only when they saw him completely did they scream, Samuel shuddered slightly, their screams still haunted him, and run away. They had run straight home, and told their parents, only one of them came, the woman, and she only believed the children when she saw him.

She had not believed them, almost like humans were fairy tales. Could that be it, in this place humans were just myths and legend? Perhaps to those people Samuel was just a monster to be slain. "The boy" Samuel whispered, "the character the insect boy had been playing was he pretending to be a human." All this would also explain their instantaneous fear and hatred of him.

They had arranged a mob to run him into the ground and set dogs on him. Had it not been for an incredible bit of luck, finding the cavern, they would have succeeded. Samuel concluded that he should keep his distance from everyone from now on.

As he walked on, his hand suddenly fell away from him. It felt as though he had missed a step. Samuel found himself near a cave. At first, he assumed that he had gone full circle and was back home, but on closer inspection, this was another cave entirely. This one was far deeper and not as high.

Inspecting the cave for any signs of another underground passage, but after turning over almost every stone for an out of place black slab, he found nothing. It was just an ordinary cave, a little disappointed he instead attempted to look for anything that could be useful. Giving every stone and pebble a thorough examination, until he discovered some flint.

"Flint" he mused to himself "that might come in handy." Samuel pocketed a few lumps of flint and left the cave. Samuel then set himself a task; he would learn how to start a fire. He jogged to the edge of the forest looking for any silver birch trees; he remembered that their bark made good tinder. Walking back in the direction he came, and after about an hour he eventually found the tree he wanted.

Carefully he peeled the papery bark of the trunk until he had stuffed his pockets with as much as they could hold. Heading back towards the extension he collected as many twigs and logs as his hands could hold. By the time he made it back home, he was tired, and his arms began to strain under the weight.

Setting his load down he arranged his arranged his sticks in a little pile and took out his flint, grabbing a nearby stone, he struck the stone attempting to create a spark. He failed no matter how hard he hit the flint or from what angle he could not produce a spark. Picking a separate piece of flint, he next tried to strike two pieces of flint together, but once again he got nothing "if only I had a knife" Samuel moaned to himself.

Samuel made attempt after attempt, but he could not get any sparks to form. Now frustrated beyond words, he threw the flint as hard as he could. The flint struck a stone on the floor. As the piece of flint shattered into dozens of small shards, a stream of sparks erupted from the rock it had landed on.

With fresh enthusiasm he dashed to the rock, it was large, around the size of Samuel's head, with streams of red running through it. Samuel brought his whole piece of flint down and hit the red streak, once again sparks came from it.

Heading off to pick up his fuel he placed his hands on the ground, and a sharp stabbing pain arose in his left hand.

Lifting his hand up he saw a shard of flint, around the size of his thumb, was sticking out of his palm. Trickles of blood oozed out of the fresh wound. Placing the fingers of his uninjured hand on the flint, he carefully pulled the foreign body out. The pain was surprisingly great for such a small injury. When it finally came free to blood began to pour out. Samuel tore off a piece of his polo shirt and wrapped it around his wound.

As he was about to throw the offending shard out of the cave entrance when he realised it could be used to cut apart the fish in the pool. Pocketing the shard, he once again moved towards the timber and dragged it towards the rock. Getting his undamaged flint, he placed the birch bark on the floor and struck the rock once again. Sparks came from the stone and landed on the tinder.

It did not, however, catch fire. The glowing orange beads faded away without ceremony or any flames emerging. Samuel struck the stone time after time after time but with no luck. The sun had climbed high into the sky and sweat was pouring from his face, this was incredibly difficult, and once again anger welled up inside him and just as he was about to pack the whole thing in the tinder glowed.

Samuel blew gently on the glowing ember, and it grew bigger. Bringing more of the bark shavings towards it and at last, the flames burst forth. Samuel kept feeding it until it became large enough to place the larger pieces of wood on. As the fire roared, Samuel sat back and admired his handiwork.

As Samuel gazed into the fire, its warmth and the gentle dancing of the flames comforting him, his stomach began to growl. Not surprising really, he had not eaten anything since the previous day. Samuel could go back to the pool and catch another fish without too much effort, but he did not want to leave his fire unattended, not because it might burn anything but because he was concerned that it might go out.

Samuel sat there weighing up his options, his own indecisiveness starting to annoy even him, in the end, his stomach made the choice for him. Pushing the slab out of the way, a gust of warm air brushed his face, and he descended into the corridor he stopped only to move the slab back in place behind him.

As he trotted down the corridor, he once more thought about the fire. He could not leave the fire burning through the night. Not just because he could not tend it 24/7, he needed sleep after all, mostly as the light would be glaringly apparent at night and draw those people to him.

A familiar blue glow appeared up ahead and once more the cavern opened up before him. Jogging towards the pool, he rolled up his right sleeve, lay down by the water's edge and placed his arm into the pool. He waited patiently as he had done before and caught another fish.

Killing it quickly with a sharp blow to the head he pulled himself up off the ground, taking care not to put pressure on his wound, the pain having been replaced with a dull ache, and suddenly realised how hard the stone floor was. Not relishing spending the night on the unforgiving rock he endeavoured to do something about it after dinner. As he reached for his most recent catch, he remembered yesterday's meal. His new home would not become a sty. Samuel picked them both up and headed back outside.

Samuel reached the steps, moved the slab and stepped yet again into the fresh air. The fire had become quite weak in his absence. Almost dashing towards his log pile he placed fresh wood onto the fire.

As the flames became healthy again he picked up the mangled fish skeleton and threw it as far as he could, it made it all the way to the forest edge. Samuel's attention was now squarely on his dinner. Not wanting another injury Samuel carefully removed the flint from his pocket and began to prepare the fish.

To begin with, he stuck the shard into the back of the fish's head. He cut around the fish's neck it was a sloppy job, and he would not have won fishmonger of the year, but it did the trick. He pulled the fish's head away from the body and its guts trailed behind it. Disgusting but it was none the less effective "I'll have to remember that trick" he said, making a mental note.

Slicing the fish's belly open he then opened it like a book. After scraping out the organs and removing the spine and as many bones as he could, Samuel picked up one of the thinner twigs. Making a few guide holes with the flint shard, he skewered his meal and carefully positioned it over the fire.

It was not long before the smell of roasting fish filled the extension. It was unbearable the wonderful smell was driving his stomach wild. Resisting the urge to ram it all into his mouth, he turned the fish around for more even cooking. As the white flesh of the fish steadily turned golden brown, he looked outside. "Hmm I hope there aren't any bears nearby," Samuel said with a slight amount of worry in his voice.

Samuel moved his meal away from the fire to let it cool slightly. The sun was beginning to set now and was starting to paint the sky orange. It had been quite a day learning how to start a fire and gut a fish; he certainly had not imagined he would be doing it last week. Samuel reached for his dinner and began to eat.

The fish yesterday had been good, but it could not compare to one that had been cooked. It was as though the flakes danced in his mouth, he had never had anything better in his life, and in fact, it was making him a little giddy.

Supremely satisfied with his meal Samuel let it settle in his stomach. Samuel remembered that he had to look for something to soften the floor for tonight, he did not have long, soon the sun would set, and he would not be caught outside after dark.

Leaving the cave, once again placing the slab back in place, he walked to the wood's edge carrying the remains of his dinner. After discarding them, he began to search the forest floor, always being careful to keep the extension within view. On the ground, there were few fallen leaves. Samuel picked them up anyway willing to except anything that would make tonight more bearable.

Samuel worked until dusk gathering fallen leaves, pulling up grass and flowers and depositing them outside his home. It was a lot of effort for relatively little gain but would have to do. After kicking the remains of his fire until not even an ember remained, he gathered up all of his bedding and climbed down into the corridor.

Finally reaching the cavern, the long walk to and from the outside world becoming a little tedious now, he placed his bedding down underneath a ledge. He spaced it out evenly creating a small, raised, area for his pillow, he lay upon it and a sharp pain stabbed into his leg. It was the flint again, but it did not cause an injury this time. Emptying his pockets and placing everything carefully beside him Samuel once again attempted to lay down on his makeshift bed.

This time was a success. It was not exactly comfortable, but it was definitely an improvement. Samuel lay there gazing up at the ceiling watching the worms crawling about, dragging their lights behind them. The glow from their tails was making his eyes heavy. Samuel thoughts began to drift on to what tomorrow would bring, would he ever meet those people again? Or was he firmly out of their territory? Would he ever get home? A slight pang of sorrow filled Samuel's chest. He let out a deep sigh that echoed throughout the cavern, this calmed him down. "One thing at a time Samuel, One thing at a time" the answers would have to come later, for now, he slept.

Chapter 4

Steam slowly rising from the pool is what met Samuel's sight as he awoke. Samuel stretched out and immediately a searing pain rocketed through his left hand. He had hit the ledge and reopened his wound. Samuel grabbed his hand and began rubbing the area around the injury trying to make the pain go away. Fresh blood seeped onto his makeshift bandage. Getting to his feet, he walked to the pool and removed the scrap of fabric from his hand, the dried blood from the previous day pulled at his skin making it even more painful, and submerged it in the water.

Small streams of blood slowly dispersed in the warm water. Eventually, the pain subsided, and he pulled his hand out. Blowing on his palm to make it dry faster Samuel thought to himself "this is quite possibly the worst morning I have ever had." Samuel also cleaned the rag by dipping it in the water and giving it a vigorous rub with his right hand Samuel did not want to get an infection out here.

As he waited for the rag to dry off, he wiped the sleep from his eyes and took a few sips of the water to remove his thirst. Sitting back down Samuel considered his options for the day. He should get something to eat but he was not feeling particularly hungry at the moment, and the fish were so docile that he could easily catch more when he felt hungry. That decided he tried to think of something else to occupy his time.

Samuel stretched again, and something wafted past his nose. He realised it was him, he had not taken a shower or bath in four days. "Well, that settles that then," said Samuel nodding as he spoke. He removed all of his clothes, laying them neatly by the water's edge, and slid into the pool.

The warm water was just a wonderful as he remembered. Its warm embrace made Samuel feel secure. Samuel swam in a small circle, well paddled really, savouring his bath. Scrubbing himself vigorously, using his nails, to make up for the lack of soap Samuel soon began to feel the accumulated dirt wash away. Feeling clean and refreshed he rested his arms on the edges of the pool, Samuel was going to have a good, long soak. "I have an indoor pool, a heated indoor pool" Samuel slapped his head for not realising sooner.

As Samuel stood there, the fish swimming around his legs, he began to think about his next move. He looked up and closed his eyes, in an attempt to help him think, he was still not hungry. Samuel felt he should get an early start on becoming more familiar with the lay of the land. He turned around and lifted himself out of the water, once again being careful not to use his left hand, Samuel walked towards a ledge that was around knee height, sat down and waited to dry off.

This was taking forever. Samuel had sat on that ledge for what felt like an hour. He tried to think of a way to speed this up, then it dawned on him hadn't he already solved this problem. Disappointed with himself he trudged his way to the dry air of the corridor. Standing there; with the dry air quickly stealing all of the moisture off his skin. When he had dried off, he dressed, reapplied his bandage and walked down the corridor.

Once he had made it to the slab, he noticed that there was no light coming through the cracks. His first thought was that someone was standing or sitting on it. Samuel froze in place trying not to make a single sound. His heart beat fiercely in his chest, had someone found the fire's remains. Listening intently for the slightest noise from above any indication for who might be up there. He heard nothing, however.

Slowly his confidence came back. He took a tentative step forward placed his arms on the slab and slowly lifted it up, ever so slightly. He saw no one, in truth he did not see much of anything, the sun had not yet risen. A great sense of relief came over; he had been worried for nothing. Moving the slab back he walked into the night. Well it was actually early morning, the sky was a deep blue, and the breeze was refreshingly cool, he examined the remains of yesterday's fire, and it was as he had left it, it remained undisturbed, that was good. No one had found him yet.

Looking up at the sky he saw a few wispy clouds hanging in the air. Samuel had headed left yesterday so this time he felt he should go right. There was a slight chill in the air, but it was not unbearable, and the blades of grass and tree leaves were covered in dew. Stepping out of the extension, he stumbled on a loose rock.

Heading off curious about what he would find today, although slightly worried he would meet his attackers again, Samuel was hoping for was a king sized bed but he would take an old blanket.

As the sun climbed higher, a dull yellow light rolled over the landscape, and Samuel began to get a better look at his surroundings. The old mountain stretched out in front as far as he could see "How big is this thing?" Samuel asked himself in slight amazement. "Perhaps this really is the remains of a mountain range," he said thinking up new answers.

The morning walk continued uneventfully for several more hours when suddenly something in the forest caught his eye. It was a tree, nothing particularly strange about that but hanging from its branches were fruit. They looked like apples, bright red, but they were huge so large that it seemed it would take two hands to hold them.

Walking towards the tree, Samuel noticed that all of the apples were tantalisingly out of reach. He tried looking for a stick to knock the fruit down but he could not see any. "Right," he said with determination I his voice "let's do this the old-fashioned way." Looking for the lowest hanging branch he jumped and held onto it, his injury complained at the sudden pressure put on it but Samuel tried his best to ignore it.

This was the easy part pulling himself up, however, was almost impossible. Samuel tried again and again, but his arms just did not have the strength to do it. Samuel, however, was not going to be beaten by a tree. He walked back to the old mountain looking for any rocks that he could throw.

He discovered plenty, picking up as many as he could Samuel then went back and selected the biggest one he could see and began to pelt the fruit. This method would bruise the fruit of course but bruised was better than nothing. He missed on his first few throws but eventually, he hit his target. Some of the apple's flesh was torn off by the impact, but it too was pulled away from the tree.

The apple hit the ground with a great thud. Samuel bent down and collected his reward. The fruit was as big and heavy as it had looked and it indeed took both his hands to hold it. Selecting a part of the apple his stone had not hit he bit into it.

It was the best apple he had ever tasted, it was sweet and moist, the texture was indescribable, even the skin which Samuel usually did not care much for was wolfed down with great relish.

Samuel ate every last piece of the apple. Supremely satisfied with his breakfast Samuel wanted more for his dinner tonight. Looking back up Samuel was suddenly struck with a realisation. He was horribly ill-equipped for this world.

He could not even climb a tree for goodness sake. Samuel had only escaped his pursuers through sheer dumb luck. Had he not found that cavern he would have been killed, if the fish had not been so docile, he would have starved. Samuel could not rely on that good luck forever.

"My body needs to become stronger" Samuel firmly told himself. He would need to exercise every day, strengthen every muscle in his body until he could climb a tree without effort, run a mile in four minutes, and wrestle one of those dogs to the ground with his bare hands.

Samuel knocked another apple to the ground. Holding it in his is hands, rubbing it, he decided he would eat it later; it would be his reward for the hard work he intended to put in. Walking to the centre of the grassy clearing Samuel rubbed his feet on the ground like an impatient horse and then ran.

Samuel ran at a steady pace. he would work on his legs, build up endurance if he ever reencountered those people he would leave them in the dust. His feet slammed against the ground, sending shockwaves up his spine, his breathing became heavy and steadily sweat began to appear.

It was slightly easier, than the chase the day before and travelling up and down the corridor having given Samuel a little practice. He was not however anywhere near the level he wanted. Samuel ran onward each step taking him further from home.

It was midday now Samuel had been running on and off all the time, Samuel decided that he deserved a break. He slumped himself down on the ground panting heavily. Samuel was happy with himself, he had indeed covered a good distance this morning. Samuel waited until his breathing slowed down and then he would jog back home. He could probably pick up some more apples on the way.

Samuel was waiting patiently when something pricked his ears. He heard sound coming from the forest. Samuel immediately became worried he stood bolt upright and focused his attention on the trees. "Maybe it's just my imagination like this morning," Samuel thought in an attempt to reassure himself.

Only this time there really was something out there, he heard it again, rustling and very faintly he heard more of that strange language. Carefully Samuel walked back in the direction of his home, keeping his eye fixed on the tree line.

As Samuel was slowly creeping along the forest edge, he heard a familiar sound. It was a high-pitched voice; he could not understand what was said, but he could tell from who it had come. It was that little Lamia from the day before, he was sure of it, and slowly Samuel walked into the forest.

Taking extra care to memorise his steps so that he could find his way back. Samuel walked slowly to the source of the sound, which stopped and started irregularly, Samuel did not know why exactly he wanted to see that girl again; after all, it made far more sense to get out of there. Samuel believed it was because he desired answers; he wanted to know precisely why that girl had screamed like she did.

The child's voice was getting louder, Samuel was getting closer, but this time, however, he did not want to be seen. Samuel poked his head around a nearby tree and there she was, he had been right. The little girl was just how Samuel had remembered golden hair and scales, the dress with the same diamond pattern. She was holding another stick, this one was a bit thicker than the one she had had before, an upgrade maybe?

She, well Samuel did not really have a word to describe how she moved, the child's snake half waved slightly side to side as she moved. Every so often she would stop and look at something on the ground, inspect it, and then carry on. It seemed as though she was looking for something.

Her friends, however, were nowhere to be seen. Samuel supposed that they had been too frightened to go out on their own again, but this child was not. Samuel was impressed by the little Lamia's courage. Samuel, of course, was no threat to her but she did not know that. "Hold on for one moment," Samuel thought "is she looking for me?"

Samuel took a few steps back to put more distance between them but still keeping the girl in view. The girl continued to move forward turning over almost every stone and leaf. If she was indeed looking for Samuel, she was vastly overestimating his abilities.

The day past [Passed] at a sedate pace, from that moment on the girl sliding forward slowly and Samuel keeping an eye on her, all the while keeping his ears pricked for the slightest sound coming from elsewhere. It was then that the girl reached the edge of the forest.

The girl stopped moving at once, she peered out into the open space and the old mountain. It did not seem that she, at any point, would make that last movement and step out. It was not long before she turned around and went back the way she had come. It would seem that not even the desire to track Samuel down would make her leave the forest.

She whacked her stick against a nearby tree trunk, she was apparently frustrated, Samuel felt it was strange that she was undeterred by being alone in a forest but was worried about being alone out in the open. Samuel supposed she must have her reasons and put it out of his mind.

Samuel had followed the girl for the best part of the day, and apart from the fact that this girl liked sticks and disliked open spaces had learned nothing. Deciding to cut his losses, and before he could no longer remember the way back, he set off home. Then suddenly another voiced erupted, and two other people appeared.

They were both adults. The first was one of those insect people, a man, around the same height as Samuel. He had crimson red hair that travelled to his shoulders and chitin on his forearms and legs were also the same shade of red, which seemed to radiate in the light. His antenna twitched furiously. He was wearing a blue tunic, with a pattern on the front, an emblem; five circles stacked one on top of the other.

Suddenly out of the blue something clicked. Those three stones he found in the forest, the symbols they had on them. A diamond, five circle and finally two triangles. Each on corresponded with a different race of these people the Lamia's had the diamond, the insectoids were the circles, and by process of elimination, the sheep people owned the triangles. "Well, that was at least one mystery solved" Samuel mused to himself.

Sheep people he had to come up with a better name than that. "Weresheep maybe" thought Samuel, "No that was seriously lacking in imagination, what kind of idiot thought that up?" "Probably some overweight idiot that still lived with his parents" Samuel chuckled inside his head. He could not think of anything else so weresheep it would have to be for now.

The insect spoke to the girl in a disapproving tone. She replied, seemingly defending herself, and waving her free hand as she did it. Interrupting her the other person spoke. This one was a woman another Lamia with golden hair and scales much like the girl, Samuel assumed that this was her mother, her hair was tied up into a ponytail that extended halfway down her back. The woman's eyes were a deep hazel and also had cat-like pupils. She wore a long dress, coloured sky blue that stopped just before the rest of her touched the ground.

The woman was really giving it to the girl, yep this was defiantly [definately] her mother, and she carried on ranting for over ten minutes before she finally calmed down. The little girl lowered her head slightly and said something, probably an apology.

The insectoid then knelt down and looked the girl in the eye and said something else, with a soft tone in his voice, the three people then turned about and headed off. Samuel then followed behind them.

Taking extra care not to be spotted Samuel crept on after them. As he did a familiar feeling appeared within him, it was the same as when we [He] had seen that weresheep woman the day before. It was something to do with the way these people looked. It was not their non-human parts that bothered him, strange as they were, it was the rest of them.

These two people were gorgeous. No other word could describe them, they looked as though they had been sculpted by a master craftsman, and that was not right. Real people had flaws; they had moles, scars and imperfections. They did not have perfect symmetry, flawless teeth and faces that could put the world's best models to shame.

The girl's free hand reached for her mother's, and they continued onward. The mood had changed rather quickly, the girl and her mother talked, smiled and laughed while the man watched on with a smile on his face.

After a short walk, the forest opened up to reveal open fields filled with wheat. The long golden stalks swayed gently to and fro in the light breeze and in the distance, Samuel saw buildings. The three people turned too, walked around the edge. Samuel took extra care this time to avoid being spotted and slowed his pace.

Up ahead was a pile of assorted objects, bits of wood, old pieces of fabric and other miscellaneous items. The people he was following barely took any notice, and Samuel was about to do the same when something shiny caught his eye. Samuel stopped following and as soon as they were out of sight, like a magpie, he went to inspect it.

Samuel reached out and lifted the object of the ground. It turned out to be a knife. The blade was about as long as Samuel's hand, it was old, slightly rusted and a bit dull with a crack running about a quarter of the way down. Samuel, however, believed he could work with it so be pocketed the old utensil.

This was a rubbish pile, anything these people had that was broken, or they did not want was just dumped here. Samuel did believe that a beggar could not be a chooser so he began rooting around for anything else he might need. After a short scrounge he found an old blanket it was a dull grey colour and a little threadbare, it needed a wash but it was still usable, as well as a pouch, made out of what he believed to be leather, brown in colour with a good shine on it, apparently it had been well looked after. It was perfectly serviceable, so Samuel tried not to imagine what had led its owner to throw it away.

Taking his newly earned spoils, Samuel walked on after the girl. It was a short walk, and Samuel finally found them again. Only now they had been joined by many more people. The other two children from the other day before were there, talking feverishly with the Lamia. Many other adults were there as well.

They talked, they frowned, they laughed and hugged, and suddenly Samuel felt incredibly lonesome. He missed his family, looking at all of these people reminded him of them. His desire for answers eclipsed, Samuel turned to head back home, taking one last look at those happy people and with teary eyes walked on.

Samuel worked on automatic slowly caressing his finger, barely aware of the world around him; thoughts of the life he had lost would not leave him alone. He finally exited the forest at almost the exact same point he had entered it, had he been in a better mood he would have admired his sense of direction.

The sun was setting, and Samuel found himself at the extension, walked down the corridor and into the cavern. Dropping his new possessions unceremoniously on the floor, the knife making a clang as it hit the stone, and slumping on his pile of grass and leaves. He considered getting something to eat, but he did not feel hungry

Lying there with memories of his family tormenting him Samuel closed his eyes just wanting the day to be over. "Why did this have to happen to me?" Samuel mumbled to himself trying to push his feeling to one side. He tossed and turned for what seemed like hours, the stress preventing him from sleeping, placing his arm over his forehead and looking upward Samuel wondered if he could ever be as happy as those people were.

Samuel did not want to feel like this, who does? He wished he could just choose not to feel, but Samuel was wise enough to know that wishes do not come true. He would have to do something about this himself; he always had to do it himself. Samuel was reminded about all of the challenges he had already triumphed over, both here and in his old life. A new emotion filled him, it flowed through his body and with a refreshed conviction his worries and sadness lessened, and Samuel's eyes became heavy.

Chapter 5

His sleep was once again peaceful, no nightmares, and Samuel could at least be grateful for that. Samuel felt strangely refreshed, he could not think of any cause of this, almost leaping to his feet Samuel decided he would face the day with all the vigour he could muster. He took off his clothes and jumped in the pool.

Samuel was not happy however, he was just determined, he had not felt even a glimmer of that emotion since the day he got here. Samuel took a deep breath and dived under the water; the fish swam lazily out of the way. He surfaced and began to swim up and down the length of the pool. He had done around ten laps; he was not keeping count.

He suddenly remembered his injury, removing his bandages he was amazed at how much it had improved in such a short amount of time there was a thick brown scab surrounded by fresh pale skin. He pressed his fingers around the healing injury; it hardly hurt at all. Believing that he no longer needed his bandage he swam to the poolside and threw it out of the water. He then began to scrub himself down; he would also ensure that he remained clean.

Hauling himself out of the water he sat down with his feet kicking around in the water. Samuel would try to swim every day. "What to do?" Samuel said emphasising each word getting dressed would be a good start. Getting up he noticed the items he had dumped yesterday. Grabbing his blanket and inspecting it again, it really did need a wash, several food stains covered it so he walked back to the pool and began to scrub the fabric a vigorously as he could. The water quickly took most of the dirt out. "Was there anything this pool could not do?" Samuel was beginning to suspect that there was something strange about his pool.

The healing of his hand had sped up after his bath, it removed stains from clothes maybe it had also been crafted like the cavern. He could not prove it, of course, it might be just a coincidence. It was just another strange occurrence in this place.

Taking the blanket and himself into the corridor to dry off he began to feel hungry. "Should I have apples or fish for breakfast?" Samuel mused to himself both were delicious and had their own unique charms. Apples he concluded. He remembered the apple he had knocked down yesterday. Samuel glanced inside it was not near his bed or the knife and pouch. He must have dropped it at some point, most likely when he had felt so depressed. No matter he would just have to go out and get another.

When he was at last dry he got himself dressed, "I should wash my clothes when I get back," and picked up his knife, the piece of flint he had put down the other day and the pouch. He discovered that the pouch had a few strands of leather coming off it, tied in a tight knot. Using the point of his knife he cut a small hole in his trousers waist. He undid the knot on the pouch and threaded it through, tying it tight.

Feeling ready to take on the outside world he walked down the corridor, as he came towards the slab Samuel noticed that weak sunlight was pouring through.

In his depression Samuel had forgotten to replace it "damn" he said livid at himself, "what if someone had come along and found it?" He could be dead right now. Walking up the steps and moving the slab back in place, his old fire caught his eye. Samuel began to wonder what roasted apples would be like; he would have to collect some more tinder and firewood while he was out.

Turning right he decided he should jog to the tree, rather than walk, and so Samuel set off to find his breakfast. Keeping a steady pace, breathing deeply, his pouch slapping against his side Samuel could already feel his efforts paying off, he could go further and harder than he ever could in his life. A great sense of satisfaction washed over him, but he knew that there was still a long way to go.

To his left he spotted the unmistakable sight of silver birch, its white bark breaking up the repetitiveness of brown and green. Stopping to fill his pouch with as much tinder as it could hold and then continued on his morning jog. Quicker than he expected Samuel reached the apple tree, his breathing was surprisingly lax considering all the effort he had put in, just another sign he was getting there.

Samuel found the low hanging branch and once again tried to climb it. He jumped his hands grasping the bark, its rough texture digging into his hands. With all of his strength, Samuel attempted to haul himself up, it was incredibly hard, but every second he pulled himself a little higher. When his chin was level with the branch, he swung his leg over it, just as he had done with the ledge in the cave.

With hindsight, Samuel probably should have practised in there, but it was too late do that now. Panting he sat on the branch, it was uncomfortable, and his face was red, but he had done it.

Now came the tough part, Samuel took a look down and was immediately struck with a sense of vertigo. He was only about two metres off the ground, but his head spun slightly and he grasped the branch tight, Samuel sat in the tree for several minutes rubbing his finger as he breathed slowly and deeply in an attempt to regain his composure.

Samuel was beginning to calm down "I hate heights" he mumbled to himself, but he could not let it stop him, not in this place, and so every so carefully Samuel turned himself around so that he was facing the trunk and gently slid himself over the bark. When he reached his goal, he placed one of his feet on the branch and holding onto the trunk lifted himself onto his feet.

His vertigo came flooding back even worse than before. He held on tight and breathed just as he had done the last time, he needed to beat this, as the spinning sensation slowed once again he looked up and saw several of the bright, plump fruit handing just within reach. Stretching his left hand out is fingers gently tickled the apple, Samuel leaned out a little further to get a firm grip. His hands closed around it, and he pulled down hard. The fruit released its grasp on the tree and came down hitting the ground with a satisfying thud. "I did it" Samuel applauded himself yet he was not entirely pleased just however. Reaching out for another apple he pulled a second then a third came down.

Deciding that that was enough for now, Samuel began the tricky business of getting down. His first idea was to sit back down and slide off, so he only had to drop a few centimetres.

Samuel, however, wanted to beat his problem not push it to one side, so with his body telling him to do anything, he jumped down. Or to be more accurate he tried to, but his legs froze up, and he just stood there. "Come on Samuel, you have jumped from higher places than this" This was true of course, but that time he had angry villagers and dogs to motivate him. The panic was making his legs shake, and his vision was blurring if he did not jump soon, he would fall.

Dredging up every ounce of courage he had Samuel was finally able to jump from the branch. It was a shortfall, but that did not prevent the massive surge of adrenaline from pumping through his veins. Samuel's heart felt as though it had leapt into his mouth. As his feet hit the floor, he felt a massive force of the impact surge through his body. His legs bent under the pressure, and he fell backwards.

As the panic began to subside Samuel raised his head and realised that he was still on his back. He had almost fainted from the ordeal, but he had succeeded. Samuel had beaten his fear, for now. Samuel relaxed his neck and let his head lie on the floor. He giggled as the hormones wore off and Samuel slowly pulled himself to his feet.

Standing tall, savouring his victory, Samuel knew that to another this would seem like a small insignificant thing but to him, it was one of the great triumphs of his life. Picking up his well-deserved reward he stood tall. His now arms full of fruit Samuel walked home.

The trip did take some time, but it was not even midday yet. Samuel placed his breakfast on a large, wide stone inside the extension and then walked back to the forest edge to look for more firewood. It did not take him long to gather up an armful of wood and carrying back he let it fall beside the food.

Removing a handful of tinder from his pouch, he placed it on the floor. Next, he took the flint from his pocket, pointing the flint towards the bark he put his knife on the flint, edge pointed down and rapidly scraped along the stone. A shower of bright yellow sparks erupted from the blade as they hit the tinder, it immediately began to smoulder, striking the flint two more time and blew gently on the embers until they turned into flames.

When the fire had grown healthy Samuel's attention turned towards his breakfast "now how am I going to do this?" he asked himself. He could just run a stick through and try to cook it whole, but he would probably end up burning it. He placed the knife over the flames to sterilise it. To be sure that he did not ruin the whole thing Samuel cut two segments out of one of the apples and put a stick through one of them, he positioned it above the fire while he ate the second piece right there and then.

The fresh apple wedge was just as good as it had been yesterday cool and crisp. As a beautiful smell of burning sugar entered his nose Samuel removed the apple from over the fire he blew on it and took a bite, and it was just as magical as he had imagined, the apple was much sweeter now it was almost like golden syrup. After eating two apples Samuel began to feel a little sick "too much sugar I suppose" said Samuel stating the obvious.

Standing up Samuel kicked ash from the previous fire into the current one. As the flames died, he pocketed the flint and picked up the remaining apple. Moving the slab, he walked down into the corridor.

Reaching the cavern, Samuel grasped something to do. He had a lot of free time, a bath, washing up, looking for breakfast, overcoming his fear, eating his meal and it was not even noon yet. He was going to wash his clothes but what after that? "Is this how every day is going to be like?"

Picking up his blanket, it had dried nicely, and a faint scent was emanating from it he could not put his finger on what it was, but it was pleasant. Samuel placed it, his knife and apple down by his bed, the distinctive smell of rotting vegetables was coming from it, he would have to replace it soon. Strolling to the pool Samuel removed his hoodie and shirt, they were heavy with sweat and dirt and proceeded to wash them with as much energy he had put into his blanket. As Samuel knelt, scrubbing away with all his might, Samuel gained a new appreciation for his mum and all the work she had put in. He also felt a fresh bout of guilt for when he had rubbed jam and chocolate sauce in-between her bed sheets.

After their scrub he took them to the corridor, "Might as well name it" mused Samuel "the dry room?" he asked himself. Yes, that was good enough, he could always rename it. Placing his clothes in the newly christened dry room, Samuel caught a glance of the diving board.

"I should jump off that" he suggested to himself. He had bested his fear earlier today, but he had not banished it entirely, and so he reasoned that if he could dive off that board without any fear or hesitation, he could dismiss it forever, plus it would give him something to do while his clothes dried. Samuel removed his trainers and socks, removing everything from his pockets, positioned them neatly on the floor, and began to climb the ledges.

Clambering over the rocks was an exciting experience, helped by the fact that unlike last time he was not in horrible pain, the ledges on the same row varied in height for no apparent reason, probably some design choice made by an architect who had never climbed anything in his life, though each row behind the last was always taller.

Samuel was travelling in the most challenging direction he could find and although his legs were still fine, his arms and back were beginning to feel the strain. The final kick in the teeth was that he was not even a quarter of the way up.

Samuel persevered however and slightly out of breath he reached the back of the diving board. Samuel was quite high up now, over three-quarters of the way to the ceiling, he could make out the faint outlines of the glow worms. Carefully walking toward the edge, determined not to slip, he peered over the edge.

The pool lay directly beneath him gentle wafts of steam slightly obscured the water. Looking straight down he saw that the pool was much larger than he had thought, larger than even an Olympic size pool. The familiar sense of disorientation started to overtake him, and Samuel took a step back. Closing his eyes and taking a deep breath Samuel rubbed his finger and tried to psyche himself up for the plunge. He told himself that he could do it, that he needed to. It made little difference however the sense of dread would not leave him.

Samuel hopped from one foot to the next, clapping his hands together, Samuel just decided to go for it. Taking a deep breath and one huge leap off the edge, he plummeted down into the warm water. He hit the water in a semi cannonball while the fish got the most tremendous shock of their lives as a five-foot-eleven-inch lump of pink meat exploded into their world.

As he slowed down, Samuel uncoiled himself and began to surface. When the fresh gulp of air hit his lungs combined with the rush of the fall was almost euphoric, "at this rate I might become an adrenaline junkie" Samuel speculated.

Taking the time to enjoy a quick swim Samuel then exited the water, shaking himself like a wet dog, content with his accomplishment. Drying off and getting dressed he moved on to the next task, replacing his bedding, it was not glamorous, but it needed doing. Wanting only to make one trip he gathered up as much of the vegetation as he could and walked down the dry room.

Back in the open air Samuel dumped the dead leaves and grasses a fair distance from the entrance and then started to pick up some fresh bedding. It was a laborious process, he had picked up almost all of the fallen leaves during his last scrounge, but it still did not take long to find enough to ensure a comfortable night.

Taking his haul back to the cavern and laying it out in the same place as before; Samuel then placed the blanket over the plant matter, giving it two quick pats, Samuel took a few steps back. "This is ridiculous, I have done everything I planned, and it isn't even dinner time," Samuel said in disbelief. He began to wonder how all those tribe's people across the world spend their free time.

His mind began to drag up memories of some old nature documentaries he had watched when he was going through a hippy phase. They had hunted and gathered, they migrated, not really an option for Samuel, they made things, weapons, clothes and pieces of art. "Well I guess everyone needs a hobby," he said to himself, he had a knife, and there was plenty of wood outside, and so with a shrug, Samuel went outside.

On the edge of the forest, Samuel picked up as many, different sized and shaped, pieces of wood as he could find and brought them back to the extension. Sitting just outside the mouth with his back leaning on a rock he selected a small twig brought his knife to it and began to carve. He was not particularly interested, but it gave him something to do.

His cuts took more and more wood off, the dull edge of the blade forced him to tear more than shave until he had shaped it down to a fine point, it was thin and short, "a needle" he said with clear disinterest. As time rolled ever onward, Samuel continued to whittle, most ended in failure and he threw them away but by the end, he had carved a simple fish hook and a rather lousy replica of his knife.

Samuel picked up the largest piece of wood he had gathered and tried to think of what to make next. It was then that the image of that Lamia child flashed across his mind. Taking his knife, he tried his best to carve an effigy of the little snake girl.

As he sat there, cutting small flecks of wood, Samuel tried to think of a reason he was fond of that little girl. She was interesting, she was half snake after all, but the same could be said for the weresheep and the insect boy. No, Samuel believed it was that she was the only person he had met since coming here that had shown him any kindness what so ever, even if it was only for a moment.

Then the memory of the other day came into view. Samuel was sure that she had been looking for him. He could not be certain but her attitude at the time did not seem like she had wanted to kill him. Maybe she wanted answers as well.

The wood began to take on a serpentine shape, the tail had a few curves, the human part was much more difficult, with a round knob for a head and two twigs jutting out at ninety-degree angles, it was rather pathetic really. He suddenly became aware of the deep orange light that surrounded him, the sun was setting, Samuel was surprised that he had been working on his sculpture for hours.

Putting the figurine in his pocket, Samuel said: "I am going back!" Tomorrow after breakfast he would visit the village once more, he knew the risks involved, but they did not bother him, pocketing his other masterpieces and getting to his feet and walking down the dry room then he entered the cavern. Samuel scooped up the apple and lay down on his bed. Taking in mouthfuls of the sweet fruit he considered his approach.

Samuel was quite sure he could find it again; even without his little guide, but what would he do when he got there. Observe was the first thing that came to mind; try to understand them, what drove them? What did they value? What did they despise? Samuel obviously but what else he would stick to the trees make sure that no one saw him; he did not need a repeat performance.

His supper was now completely gone, and he lay on his side. The blanket was actually very soft and pleasant against his skin, the fabric made him feel secure, and it was not long before he was asleep.

He was in the forest; a gentle breeze licked his face and rustled the leaves, walking towards a light in the distance Samuel emerged into a clearing. It looked familiar then behind him he heard giggling. He turned to see the Lamia girl dozens of them all playing together, he called out to them, but they ignored him. Samuel reached out to touch the nearest one, but his hand passed straight through her.

Suddenly they all turned in unison to face Samuel, and together they said: "Your attempts are futile, you can never belong!"

The next thing he knew he was back in his room, his game controller firmly in his hand, a bad dream that was all, it had been a long, very long, nightmare, he looked back up at his TV screen and staring back at him through the glass was a giant glow worm. "Huh, I don't remember buying this one" he spoke aloud in confusion. Without a mouth the worm talked to him however Samuel could not understand, it used the same language as the hybrids.

Chapter 6

Faint blue lights slowly moving in the sky is what he saw next. Samuel was lying on a bed of grass and leaves. Staring upward in confusion it eventually dawned on him that he was finally awake. Breathing a sigh of relief that it was finally over he sat up.

Samuel got up, removed his clothes, did a few quick stretches and slipped into the pool. He swam several laps until he was slightly out of breath. To finish, Samuel climbed the ledges and jumped off the diving board. After drying himself off in the dry room, he picked up his trousers and the works of art he had carved yesterday fell out of his pockets.

Samuel finished getting dressed and then gathered up all of his carvings and walked to the ledge where he kept the mementoes of his old life. He placed them down until only the little figurine was left, staring at it he said in a hushed voice "gosh you are ugly" laughing inside at his own craftsmanship. He was going to place it down until an urge came over him to pocket it.

His eyes returned to his phone, holding it in his hand memories began to surface, the time he had gotten into a fight with that jerk at school, the day he had managed to trick his mom into thinking he was sick and the boring Christmas dinners he used to spend with the family that irritated him so.

At that moment Samuel would have given just about anything to experience one of those stressful, argumentative, comforting days, just once more, but standing here being upset and feeling sorry for himself would not change anything. He placed the phone back and pushed the memories from his mind, he needed some breakfast.

He caught a fish and went to the extension, on his way collecting his knife, starting a fire with some of the tinder in his pouch and the firewood that was left over from the other day. Preparing the fish, his skills had improved it looked much neater than the last time, he waited for his breakfast to cook as he gazed out at the forest, slightly tricky to see in the early morning sun, and he felt that same sense of wrongness that always emanated from it.

Then he saw it, he saw what was wrong with the forest, he stood up and practically skipped to the trees. He then walked from the tree he stood at to the one on its right, four and a half steps; he then walked to the next tree, four and a half steps, and the next tree and the one after that each tree was precisely four and a half steps from the last. This forest had not grown it had been planted, the entire forest.

It was, however, more than that, this forest had to be hundreds of years old, some of the trees in it were enormous, but they always grew four and a half steps away from each other. How was this possible? How could anyone engineer a forest that grew in perfect symmetry?

Then there were the flowers "of course" he said to himself "flowers do not grow around the base of trees, there is not enough light." So the question now was who had made this forest? This was becoming irksome every answer just yielded more questions.

It was then that the smell of burning meat hit his nose. "Bugger" he yelled and dashed towards his breakfast. The lower portion was charred black and inedible, but the rest was still fine. Tucking into his hot meal he thought about the trees, why would anyone go to that much trouble to grow a forest? It made no sense.

Disposing of the remains of his breakfast he recalled what he had told himself that he would visit the village and so Samuel headed right. On his walk, he considered again why these people hated him so much. Maybe it was merely the fact that Samuel was just too different, perhaps to them, he looked like some strange chimaera, made up from the body parts of a dozen different species.

He passed the apple tree, he considered picking up an apple for lunch, but he decided that he would need both his hands-free, so he was around three-quarters of the way there. It was still early morning; the sun was still low in the sky, so he had plenty of time to observe these people.

He was confident that he had arrived at the spot that he had entered the day before. Moving into the forest, he began to slowly make his way along what he thought was the right path. Walking inside the symmetrical forest he came across another silver birch, he quickly gathered up some fresh tinder.

Samuel had been in the forest for quite some time and was confident that he should have been there by now, he was getting a little worried. Had he made a wrong turn somewhere, he did not want to get lost in here, he closed his eyes and took in a breath and rubbed his finger to calm himself down. Samuel stood there with his eyes closed until he was able to make out a faint noise. It was the sound of people.

"Well that's a relief" he spoke in a hushed voice. Heading towards the noise he rediscovered the golden wheat fields, still dancing in the breeze, but he had come out of the forest in a different spot. He was closer to the village than before, and from here he could make out the basic shape of the buildings. They had slanted roofs and were tall, possibly two stories [storey], in the field he saw a form moving through it.

Samuel took a few steps back into the cover of the trees. He could just make out what he was, it was a weresheep, a man. Samuel felt that he was slightly taller than him, though he could not be sure, and he had far larger horns on his head than the woman had. In his hand, he held a pole of some kind, but Samuel could not tell what it was.

The man began to walk away from him, and Samuels's attention returned to the village. He started to walk closer, and the buildings came into view, they were fashioned from wood and had thatched roofs. They were indeed two stories tall, and they had large windows covered by crossed wooden beams, most likely to keep the heat in.

He moved on until he saw a gap in the buildings, it was most likely the main street of some description, the road was cobbled, and the whole place had an old English village charm about it. Then the saw them: dozens of them - Lamias, insectoids and weresheep of every size and colour. All of them were going about their business, some were trading, others chatting, a few of them argued amongst themselves.

He watched a few people walk around and stand in front of the stalls. The stall owner and customer would chat for a while until an item was handed over and the customer headed for pastures new. What was strange was that nothing appeared to have been exchanged, no money changed hands they had not even traded for it, why did the traders just give their stuff away?

Samuel was trying to sus it out when he was able to make out somebody familiar, it was an insectoid man, with blue chitin on his arms and legs, and wrapped around his head was a bandage it was the same man who had tackled him in the forest. He held his jaw, Samuel had apparently done quite a bit of damage, and a slight sense of superiority came over him.

Following the man was a large black dog, with a patch over its left eye, its owner placed his hand over its snout to make her stop, and the injured man began to talk to a male Lamia.

This man had black hair, with scales to match, Samuel had started to make out a pattern the colour of these people's hair correlated with the colour of their nonhuman parts.

The Lamia man had jet black hair, and thus his tail was the same colour. Wearing a blue top that almost touched the floor.

The two men continued to talk, while the dog sat at its master's feet, the Lamia man pointed to the injury and gave a cocky smirk. The insectoid snapped at him, with a slur in his voice, all the while giving the Lamia a stern look. The Lamia placed his hand on the insectoid's shoulder and spoke in an apologetic tone. The insectoid patted the Lamia's shoulder and did his best to smile.

Samuel began to feel a little guilty for the injury he had inflicted on this man and his dog, but in all fairness, they had tried to kill him. Samuel was becoming a little edgy with that dog sitting there, he was concerned that if he stayed here much longer it would sniff him out, so he began to move right again, leaving the crowd of people behind.

He passed another three buildings without seeing anyone else. Up ahead he could see a building more substantial than any of the others, it was two stories tall and made from stone with a thatch roof. The rock was a light grey in colour and had an extremely rough texture. The building had large windows without and beams covering them. He could make out a large door, right in the centre, large enough for four people to walk through side by side. The building also had a large clearing in front of it.

He wanted to get a closer look, it was an impressive structure, but he could not risk being spotted. Samuel thought that it could be some kind of temple or possibly it might have been a village hall where meetings took place.

Samuel walked on until he could see the back of the building it had a few windows but no secondary entrance or emergency exit. "Well that is a fire hazard," Samuel said in a disapproving tone. Further behind this building was more fields, this time filled with some kind of vegetable, potatoes or carrots probably, he could not tell Samuel was not a farmer.

Samuel stopped for a second considering if he should steal a couple of them but he found that he could not do it, *taking* these peoples rubbish was one thing, but Samuel was no thief. He walked on around the boundary of the field; the chattering of the villagers was becoming fainter, the field stretched out for what appeared to be miles. Samuel admired the amount of effort that had gone into it.

Walking for quite some time, until around noon, when Samuel noticed a new set of buildings appear before him, he glanced to his left and saw the large stone building from before. He had made a lap of the field far faster than he expected. Samuel walked closer and noticed a villager was walking towards him. Samuel took a few steps back, deeper into the forest. This person was an insectoid, a woman this time, "haven't seen one of those yet" he whispered.

She had bright purple hair with chitin to match, and like all the others she was stunningly beautiful, she wore a simple tunic a dull brown in colour, and this was strange, everyone else he had seen wore bright clothes. "She was probably just different" Samuel concluded. The woman examined the crops, occasionally talking to herself perhaps taking mental notes, at one point she ripped a plant straight from the ground.

The vegetable was, in fact, a parsnip except for the fact that it was the length of her arm. The size of the root vegetable was not however what impressed Samuel, it was the fact that she had torn it from the ground with only one arm. "I probably should not get on her bad side," Samuel told himself. The woman dropped the vegetable where she stood and then walked off inspecting the other crops.

When she was finally out of sight, Samuel checked to see if anyone one else was coming, and he walked out into the field. He found the discarded parsnip seeing if he could salvage it. Unfortunately, when Samuel picked it up, he discovered that its leaves were covered with some kind of white, powdery fungus. Samuel dropped it, a little frustrated, and decided that from now on he should accept the expert opinion of an experienced farmer.

Returning to the cover of the forest he continued to move towards the village. When he reached the first building, he found that it was similar to the other wooden buildings, except that this one was far larger and had much smaller windows.

Samuel could see now way of entering the building from this side, so he moved further onward. Faint lowing could be heard further ahead. When Samuel finally reached the corner of the structure, he saw the source of the noise.

He was now at a farmyard filled with a multitude of different animals, some familiar like cows and sheep kept in individual pens, all of them quite spacious. Samuel felt it was strange that they should keep sheep considering that some of them were, in fact, part sheep, and then he remembered a story about bushmeat he had seen on television about people eating monkeys and chimpanzees, he supposed that this situation was a lot like that. However, amongst the pigs, he saw more exotic creatures.

Ostriches, kangaroos and camels were part of this strange farm. All of the animals were large and healthy, as far as Samuel could tell, and a few were followed by their infants that bleated and grunted after their parents. Samuel was curious as to where in the world he was, to have both sheep and kangaroos was undoubtedly strange and did not match anywhere he knew of.

"Just another mystery to mull over" as Samuel mused this over in his head, another villager came along. This person was a male weresheep, black wool covered his chest, and the large silvery horns that came from his head almost shined in the sunlight, and of course, he was very handsome.

The man wore a simple grey tunic that came down to his knees, he did not wear any shoes apparently, nobody did here. He was carrying a large wooden bucket filled with some kind of diced vegetable.

The weresheep moved towards the cows, which started to make a large amount of noise and walked rapidly towards him, he emptied the bucket into a trough and the cows fought amongst themselves for the best spot. The weresheep looked intently at the cows for some time until he appeared satisfied. The man then headed towards the large building and opened a small side door, slightly obscured by the animals, after around five minutes he re-emerged with a full bucket "ahh" Samuel whispered, "it is a storehouse."

Samuel stood watching the man feed his livestock one by one and always waited afterwards to inspect the animals. Although he would have never imagined it, Samuel actually found that watching a farmer work was in fact quite interesting. Then a voice called out in the distance, the sudden shout had made Samuel jump, Samuel looked in the direction of the sound, it was the insectoid woman.

She walked up towards the weresheep held him tight and gave him a deep, long kiss. Samuel's cheeks flushed bright red so that he practically glowed, all the while feeling a little embarrassed and slightly ashamed of being present for this intimate moment. The man said something that made the woman smile and then the couple held each other's hand and walked off towards the village.

Samuel turned away from the barnyard and faced the forest. Slumping down against a tree Samuel began to process what he had just seen. Two members of a different species were in love. How did that work? It was not the fact that they looked different; Samuel could not care less about that, what made him wonder most of all was how did it work? Such as could the woman become pregnant? If she did, what would the baby look like? Would it be some kind of hybrid?

This was unlikely as he had seen no hybrids, well different hybrids, in the village. Maybe those two were hiding their relationship however it did not seem as though that there was any kind of segregation amongst the different races. He also remembered enough from biology that it was almost entirely impossible for one species to give birth to another that was so radically different physically. In short, he did not have any answers.

Standing back up he continued to walk along the outskirts for only a few more minutes until he returned to the village. This was a quieter part of this settlement, the houses were further apart, but the design was the same. He saw a few children playing together and some adults tending to the buildings. Samuel believed that this was the residential district, whereas the other part was more of a market area.

Samuel began to watch the people go about their business, completely unaware of him until he spotted another familiar face. She was another weresheep, with wool whiter than a cloud, ridged black horns adorned her head, and her hair was cut short with ribbons dotted throughout, and she was more beautiful than the sun, it was her, the little weresheep girl's mother.

She was sitting outside a house with a variety of flowers surrounding the building. The woman sat on a chair and was busy sowing a garment together. Occasionally she would look up to watch the children play, and a warm smile would wash over her face. It was quite hard for Samuel to believe that just a few days ago she had gathered a posy to hunt him down.

Amongst the children, he saw another pair of familiar faces. A young insectoid boy with jet black hair also a young weresheep with white wool and cute ribbons in her hair these two were playing with a group of three other children. It was odd that the other one was not with them. Samuel was also familiar with the game they were playing.

A young Lamia boy stood in front of the other holding a stick, with a look of vicious determination, all the while the other spoke with righteous vigour. It appeared that Samuel's appearance had caused more of a stir than he thought. As they continued to playtime seemed to slow down, and all of the terrible events that had occurred to him seemed to evaporate. Suddenly one of the children pointed in Samuel's direction. Quickly Samuel pulled himself behind the nearest tree.

His breathing started to become heavy and a sharp bitter taste shot through his mouth. He could hear the children's voices growing more frantic, and some of them let out loud cries. He stood there as a discussion went on behind him; he dared not look behind to get a look in case that anyone spotted him, after what seemed like forever the talking became quiet.

Samuel took a quick peek out from behind the tree and found that the villagers had continued on as usual. For once in his life, Samuel was glad that no one listened to children, even when they knew that Samuel was out there. He decided not to tempt fate and moved on. He passed a few more buildings but encountered no one else until he finally returned the wheat fields.

It was a short walk until he spotted the rubbish pile, to be more accurate he sniffed it out, Samuel started to inspect it for any new items he might find useful. Poking and prodding through the organic refuse he stumbled upon a bottle made out of clay or some kind of pottery, but when he lifted it up, he discovered that the bottom was missing. Very annoyed he threw it away, it shattered rather loudly, Samuel was worried that somebody might have heard him and so he hurried away; it was about time he headed home.

He found the area in which he had emerged this morning and re-entered the forest. He kept a lookout even now, paying more attention to his sense of hearing, just in case he ran into any unsavoury types. Samuel passed by tree after tree, but found no signs of any marauding demi-humans.

The journey was becoming rather boring when he saw something of particular interest, another fruit tree, only this time it was filled with oranges. "Oranges? Well, this just keeps getting stranger, where in the world am I?" Samuel exclaimed in confusion. Although Samuel did welcome the chance for some variety in his diet, the apples and fish were delicious, but he had started to become a little bored with them, so like with the apple tree he found the lowest hanging branch and attempted the climb.

Clinging onto the bough he lifted himself up, it was undoubtedly becoming easier all that swimming was paying off, and then he stood erect. Directly above him, just within reach, was a plump orange. Samuel reached out his left hand and pulled on it, it was reasonably difficult to remove it, the orange seemed quite attached to its tree, eventually, however, he was able to pull it free.

He bent his knees, and without looking, Samuel jumped off the branch and landed hard on the ground. He did, however, manage to land on his feet this time, well almost, his knees just skimmed the ground, but Samuel was content with this and continued on home.

Inspecting his prize for any signs of disease or infestation he was able to see that it was an impressive orange only just small enough to fit in his hand with stunning colour. There was nothing wrong with it, no bruises or black parts, so he started to remove the skin.

It peeled away remarkably easily, while a wonderful citrus smell emanated from it, he was about to throw the peel away when he thought that it might be able to use it as zest for his fish, so he pocketed it instead. He took the largest wedge and pulled it away from the rest. As he took that first bite, he was almost thrown back by an astonishing combination of sweetness perfectly balanced by the underlying tang. Samuel ate every last piece in quick succession.

The sun was beginning to travel lower in the sky, and the light under the canopy was becoming weaker. He was not, however, worried Samuel was sure he was almost out of the forest, and that he would be home before sunset. His thoughts once again found themselves drifting to the Lamia girl; he had not seen her all day. It was entirely possible that she had just been in a different part of the village or possibly in its centre, but Samuel believed that she had been in the woods again looking for him.

Samuel wondered what he would do if he did meet her again. If Samuel could make her realise that he did not want to hurt them, he did not think it likely, after all they did not even speak the same language. No, she would probably run off again and gather the posy and Samuel would find himself once again running for his life.

Suddenly the forest gave way to open space, he was out, and to his right, he could make out the unmistakable red shine of the apple tree. Samuel walked along the forest edge his body began to feel remarkably tired as the steadily weakening light told him it was time for bed, his feet became heavy, and his movements were sluggish, the day had apparently taken more out of him than he had realised. When the sun was just above the horizon, Samuel had finally reached home. He moved the slab aside and walked down to the dry room.

He did not even bother to remove his shoes or undo his pouch, he just slumped down on his bed, as he laid down the worms above him continued to wriggle and the fish in the pool swam and almost immediately he was fast asleep. If he had known what would happen to him tomorrow and what it would do to him, he would have had nightmares again.

Chapter 7

Samuel awoke fresh and ready for the day, standing up and stretching he then removed his clothes and began his routine of bathing, swimming and then a quick dive off the board. Below the surface of the water under the fish, Samuel saw a peculiar line running along the length of the pool. Samuel took in a lung full of air and dove underwater. Keeping his eyes open was difficult as the warm water tickled his eyes, but he did his best.

Samuel swam closer and began to feel a slight current pushing against his body; the water at the bottom was also a little warmer than the water open at the surface. Samuel swam a good six metres down, and as he got closer he stretched out his hand to feel the crack in his pool but had to pull it away before he was able to touch it, the water was far too hot, almost at boiling point; Samuel was certain he had found the source of his pool.

His chest began to feel tight, while Samuel's lungs started to burn from the lack of oxygen and Samuel began to swim rapidly towards the surface. When he broke through the water, he took in a sharp breath. Samuel relaxed and began to float on his back. Lying there steadily bobbing on the surface he felt remarkably at peace also slightly drowsy, and he might have slept there if his stomach had not spoken up.

Next, he caught a fish, and it was cooked in the extension, using a few fine shavings of orange peel to see if it would make a difference, it was good the fish seemed to absorb the orange into every part of it. As his breakfast was settling in his stomach, Samuel began to think about the day ahead. He considered going back to the village, but considering what had happened yesterday he advised himself against it.

So he decided that he would just gather some resources and spend his time relaxing, perhaps he would work on his carvings. "Yes that's a good idea" Samuel confirmed with himself, so he picked himself up and began to gather some fresh bedding. After he had an armful, he re-entered his cave and then replaced the old bedding with the new and took the old back outside.

He then felt that he should collect a handful of fruit, enough for several days at least, this would probably take most of the day and so keep him busy. Samuel walked on to find the apple tree, and he would gather enough for a feast. He walked at a slow pace taking as much time as he could, today would be a lazy day, by the time Samuel had reached the tree he was very relaxed and surprisingly content.

Samuel hauled himself up the tree and was able to bring down three fine examples of the enormous fruit, after jumping down he cradled them in his arms and headed back home by the time he made it back it was just after noon, and he placed them down on a ledge in the cavern and then headed back outside.

A taste appeared in his mouth it took a while for him to pin it down but his mind finally realised what it was, it was the citrus taste of oranges, with this new craving nagging away at him he set off to satisfy it.

The day was wonderfully calm, a slight breeze brushed his face, the sun warmed his body, and above him, birds danced in the sky and chirped away. Samuel felt a great wave of calmness washed over him, the otherness of the forest had almost wholly vanished since he figured out that it was man-made now it was just weird.

Samuel tried to think of the motive behind growing a forest that was perfectly symmetrical. Yet after putting as much brain power behind the problem as he could, without forgetting to breathe, the only reason he could think of, the only reason he would do this, was to show off, just to prove that he could, a giant 'screw you' to somebody who had pulled his hair fifteen years ago. "Somebody clearly had too much time on his hands," he said to the sky.

Samuel wondered if the villages had been the ones who grew the woods. He did not think so however, as that level of design would require bioengineering skills that those people just did not possess. "Are they even aware that this forest is not natural?" Samuel asked himself. He supposed that if they had all grown up with a forest arranged like this, then they probably would not notice.

Casting this line of thought away he realised that he had overshot the point he should have entered the forest and had to double back. This was not really a significant problem, but Samuel still kicked himself for it. He could not afford to become complacent, not here, it could get him killed.

He entered the forest slightly to the right of where he exited last night, Samuel did this because he had a feeling that he had drifted to the left as he walked, and to save him a little time. Samuel had become much better at moving through the trees, his understanding of how the forest was arranged made navigation much more manageable, he almost glided from trunk to trunk.

Samuel passed a small rocky outcrop it was arranged in a rough semicircle, he would have to remember where this was. If he ended up in there while being chased there would be no way out. Samuel moved past it without much thought until at last, he reached the orange tree.

He was about to climb up when he saw that he had picked off the only oranges within reach, Samuel would have to climb higher if he wanted more. "Well at least it's good practice" he mumbled and giving his finger a quick rub Samuel hauled himself up the tree. As he stood up on the low hanging branch he looked around for the next one he could climb up. This presented a new problem however he would have to jump to reach it.

"If it's not one thing it's another" Samuel moaned. He tried his best to work up his courage, but Samuel knew that it was going to take some time. He stood there for hours flexing his leg muscles until Samuel finally gathered all the motivation he needed and, with no small amount of fear, leapt.

His arms extended in front of his body and Samuel's hands clasped around the branch. As his body began to fall away, his arms were almost wrenched out of their sockets, but Samuel held on and started to pull himself up. Samuel arranged himself so that he was sitting on the branch. Now that he was here he realised that it was much thinner than he had supposed and became a little worried that it would not support his weight for long.

Samuel stood up while the branch creaked beneath him. Samuel slowed his breathing and focused much of his attention on keeping his balance. Samuel extended his hand and clasped his right hand around an orange, all the while steadying himself with the tree trunk. As his grip tightened around the fruit, he lost his footing and fell...

A great fear filled Samuel, he actually believed that he was going to die, his vision became blurry, and suddenly images flashed in front of his eyes, some of his home, other visions were of his family, he heard the sound of his brother laughing, and he tasted ice cream. With a large thud and a sharp pain in his back, he hit the ground.

The world became black, and all Samuel could feel was pain, for a second he actually thought he had been sent to hell, his brain tried to think of the reason he had been sent here when a light appeared before him. The light gradually grew brighter, and shapes began to form green leaves, brown branches and orange, well oranges.

He was not dead, he was not in hell, his vision had just been shaken, and Samuel felt the highest sense of relief he had ever felt in his entire life. He tried to move and let out a huge "AHHHH!" the pain in his back was very severe, but he still savoured every breath he took.

When his breathing had returned to normal he sat up, the pain was leaving him, but it was still tricky. He placed his hand on the back of his head. Fortunately, he felt no blood, neither did it hurt; this was good the last thing he needed was a concussion. Next, he felt his back and suddenly a shard of pain rocket up his body, but he could still move, so he did not think that he had a spinal injury.

He got to his feet and looked around for his orange. He found that it had rolled a good twenty metres away, so he picked both it and himself up. Deciding that falling out of a tree once was enough for today. So at a steady pace, his back slowing him down Samuel headed home.

Each step aggravated his back, and Samuel believed that he might have fractured some of his bones. As he came back to the stone semicircle a particularly bad stab of pain forced him to drop his orange "damn" he muttered and went to pick it up. Then Samuel heard a faint gasp to his right, he turned his head slowly, and a young girl appeared in his sight. She was around ten years old, with golden hair and a snake's tail below her waist covered in marvellous scales.

She did not scream this time. No, the young girl just stood there staring at Samuel all the while he stared right back, it was as though each was much too afraid of the other to move. That was until the Lamia began to retreat ever so slowly until her back was against the wall. In her hand was a familiar item a large stick of wood brandished ever so slightly as a weapon. There was no way for her to escape and it appeared to Samuel as though she was preparing for a fight.

Samuel could tell that she was afraid, the look on her face was undeniable, Samuel wanted to rush up to her, to shake her, to yell at her until she gave him answers. However, he remembered how well that had gone last time, so all he did was pull himself to his full height and continued to gaze at her.

The two of them stayed like that for what seemed an age, neither of them moving an inch, a cocktail of terrible emotions was surging through Samuel body. Even now she still hated him, she was terrified of him, and he hated it. Rage was gnawing away at his mind; resentment at this treatment was making him feel frustrated and the despair at how prophetic his nightmare had been.

If he could have seen himself at that moment Samuel would have been afraid of himself too, a small part of him wanted to hurt her for what she and these people were doing to him, that he did not act on these emotions. No Samuel knew who he was and he could never hurt a child, even one that was half snake. So he sucked in a massive lung full of air, the girl flinched at the noise, counted to ten and then breathed out again.

"I don't know why you are so afraid me," said Samuel speaking in the calmest tone he could muster "I don't know why you hate me so much, but I will not hurt you." "There is no force in existence that could make me." He paused for a few seconds and then added: "I wonder what exactly you afraid of." He said to himself more than her "is it me specifically or is it all of my kind." "Maybe there are other humans out there, and possibly they can tell me what has happened."

The girl, of course, did not understand she just stood there shaking ever so slightly. His sight turned away from the girl, and he looked up at the canopy. Through the leaves, he could just make out the sky, that brilliant blue blanket and something was comforting about it, something familiar, and at that moment he had an epiphany.

He looked back at the girl, his eyes focused directly at hers and said: "you think that I am monster don't you." "I can see it in your eyes." "But I am not, and I will prove it to you." With those final words, Samuel turned around and walked away.

Samuel did not say or think anything on his journey home his mind was utterly blank. The pain in his back was still there but even though it hurt it did hinder him in any way. He slogged through the tree almost entirely blind to the world around him. When he finally made it back he moved the slab, without replacing it, he walked down the dry room into the cavern and just lay on his bed and did not move at all until the next day.

Chapter 8

From that day onward Samuel began to change. Time moved at a glacial pace, his food became bland, and nothing interested him anymore. The only reason he ate was because he forced himself to, as though he had some kind of obligation to stay alive. The only reason he swam was because Samuel made himself do it, though it was difficult to describe what he did as swimming, Samuel just kind of doggy paddled and flailed around and it seemed that to Samuel life just was not worth living anymore.

This was not the only problem he had begun to see things, sometimes his parents would sit on the ledges and speak to him, but the only things that came out of their mouths was the same sound TV static made. while on other occasions the villagers would walk through the caverns and point and laugh. He also heard strange noises that seemed to come from everywhere, the sound was difficult to describe, sort of mix of birdsong and traffic noise, and every now and then he thought that he could hear words in-between the white noise but every time he tried to focus his attention on it or looked back at the apparitions they vanished. It might have been maddening if Samuel was not too apathetic to care.

Samuel was becoming lethargic, and he and he rarely did anything this gave him a lot of time with his thought, and he supposed that these occurrences were all because of his prolonged isolation, the lack of human contact was slowly eating away at him, he might even forget how to read, talk and even know who he was. At this point, however, Samuel considered that a blessing.

Day after day passed like this and for everyone that went by the hallucinations became more vivid, the villagers taunting became louder and more frequent. He was beginning to become severely depressed, it was as if a deep weight was inside his chest and stomach, his limbs became heavier and more than once he considered ending it all.

On occasion he would walk outside and sit in the extension with his back against the wall staring at the clouds rolling overhead for hours on end and he felt a familiar sense of envy, the same he had felt when he had watched those dragonflies dance above the stream, just like those insects, clouds had no worries.

He wondered what they were doing right now, they were either still darting back and forth across the water, or they were dead, but it did not matter which, they still did not have a care in the world.

Then after one unusually long session of cloud watching, after the sun had gone down, he saw an orange haze on the horizon. Samuel's face turned to look directly at it. "Huh," he said without much interest "the sun has come back up." His mind had slowed down to a crawl, and it took him some time to work out what it truly was. It was fire, a colossal fire.

Samuel stood up slowly to his full height and leaned against the old mountain. In the glow, he could make out thick black smoke that occasionally blotted the light out. Samuel tried to fob it off as nothing more than a bonfire, perhaps a celebration of some kind or holiday, but somehow Samuel knew that this was not the case.

The village was burning, he just knew it, and Samuel did not really care. He was just going to ignore it. He walked to the extension and took the steps down. He thought he had at least, but Samuel found himself rooted on the spot.

Something was stopping Samuel from just walking away, something deep at his core, and he knew what it was. Samuel was always loyal to himself, he did what he believed in no matter what anyone else said. No matter the cost, even if it killed him. This was the principle that he lived by, it was this that had stopped him from lashing out at that little girl a few weeks ago.

Those villagers all thought that he was a monster, but Samuel knew the meaning of monster. A monster would ignore this, a monster would leave them to their fate and Samuel was not a monster.

Samuel turned to face the fire, he did not honestly think that his presence would change anything, hell they would almost certainly kill him if they found him there, and they would blame him for this as well, but if there was any possibility that he could help anyone, no matter how small, he had to take it. Samuel was always loyal to himself.

Samuel ran towards the village as fast as he could. Entering the forest, he saw that the fire was so bright that it was visible even when obscured by the trees. His heart began to pound his chest, his breathing became rapid as his feet hammered against the ground and with every second he drew closer.

As Samuel ran, he tried to think about what he would actually do when he got there. He probably should try not to be seen, not as much for his own safety as everyone else's, if they caught sight of him they would try to drive him away and every second focused on him was a second they were not helping each other.

As he darted between the trees the light became brighter, and Samuel began to panic "I am probably going to die" he whispered to himself. However, he did not slow down.

When the trees finally gave way to a blistering inferno, it was like those old renaissance paintings of hell, the wheat fields were on fire he could see a few people trying combat the flames here, but Samuel could do nothing to help. The buildings in the distance were also ablaze, so Samuel moved closer.

The heat from the fire was extremely uncomfortable, it was making his skin sting, Samuel was around ten metres from the fire but it so intense he could not get much closer. "How did this happen," Samuel asked himself in confusion, it was as if some had set off some napalm.

He could hear upraised voices and screaming coming from in-between the houses and he could see a few frantic people darting to and fro. They were all afraid, and they were trying their best to save as much of their lives as they could.

He could see people gathering dirt with their bare hands and throwing it onto the fires, but it did not seem to be helping, the fire was just too intense. When they had thrown their handful, they dashed off to get more. Samuel looked around frantically for something that he could do to help. To his left, he saw a bunch of empty buckets the villagers were just leaving them empty instead of filling them with dirt to throw on the fire.

So Samuel had an idea. He checked to be certain that no one would see him and as quickly as he could he dashed out and grabbed every single bucket, seven in total, and began to fill them with dirt.

After he had filled every single one, he decided to take a calculated risk. He had to leave these buckets in places they would be found. He had noticed that the village followed a specific path. Samuel waited for a gap to appear in the traffic.

He had to wait for a blue-haired Lamia man to dash by, after that there would be a long enough gap for him to make his move. Two weresheep went past, then a different Lamia, until he saw his moment. The blue haired Lamia wriggled past, and so Samuel rushed out to the street. The heat was even more intense between the buildings; in fact, Samuel was sure that his hair was beginning to smoulder.

Samuel placed the buckets down as gently as he could, but he could not make it pretty, one of them tipped over and the earth it contained spilt onto the ground, but he did not have the time to fill it back up. He saw a glimpse of someone coming towards him, and Samuel hurried away back into the forest.

When he was back in the safety of the trees, he stayed to see if they would accept his help. A brunette insectoid woman was rushing back to gather more earth, but she stopped when she saw the buckets. She gave a quick look around and then picked one of them up and ran off. It was not much longer until more people came past to pick up the filled buckets. Samuel, however, knew he had truly succeeded when he saw the same brunette woman run past with an empty one.

Samuel could tell that there was something wrong. The villagers were not trying to put out the fires in the market district; they were taking all this soil elsewhere. The most likely explanation was that somebody was trapped, it was good to think these people had their priorities straight.

Samuel moved on to see if he could do anything else, he passed several more streets each one a blistering inferno, the heat was starting to suck the moisture straight out of him, Samuel was sweating profusely and incredibly thirsty, but he could do nothing about it right now.

He came up to the large stone building and finally discovered what they were trying to save. The building roof was on fire, and he could hear screams coming from the large hall. The door was burning, and the villagers that were fortunate enough to be outside were attempting to put it out. Samuel had known that this building was a death trap and he hated being right.

It did not seem that they needed his help though, the flames around the door were beginning to die. He moved on and walk down the back of the stone building, the fields behind it had escaped the fires, but the ones nearest to the village did appear to be charred. He walked along its length, the stones were warm to the touch, and he hoped that everyone inside was going to be alright.

He came to the end and saw a large gap between him and the next building if he was not mistaken it was the farmyard, he was not keen to spend so long out in the open, but if Samuel remained here, he would almost certainly be found. Samuel took the same stance as an athlete sprinter and then ran as fast as he could.

Samuel ran faster than he ever had before, the world around him turned into a blur as the farmyard came towards him at an astonishing speed. He reached the storehouse without anyone noticing him, but he was greeted by the panicked cries of animals.

The cattle lowed, the pigs squealed, the camels... made a sound Samuel could not really describe. The storeroom had escaped the rest of the blaze but the fire was terrifying the animals, some of them were banging into their fences in a desperate attempt to escape, but two people were doing their best to calm them down. Their faces were familiar it was the couple he had seen a few weeks ago in his second trip to the village. It was difficult with just the two of them, and they were just as frantic as their livestock.

The insectoid woman was removing the infant animals away from the others and putting them in separate pens, in an attempt to avoid them being crushed by the adults, but this was making the babies and mothers even more anxious. It was a catch twenty-two situation, but Samuel could not help these people either no matter how much he wanted to.

Samuel headed for the residential district, the flames had spread even here, despite the excellent distance each house had from its neighbour. Samuel could see why the wind was particularly strong tonight and it was blowing the flames to the next house along.

He noticed three people crowded around one house, in particular, they were trying their hardest to get inside. He recognised these people. It was the weresheep and Lamia girl's mothers, as well as a third he did not know, another weresheep man, taller than the weresheep mother with large silvery horns that glittered in the firelight, he had white fur on his body and was wearing a blue tunic.

The three people were screaming into the house, there was apparently someone was trapped in there as well, but amongst the horrific yells of the adults Samuel was able to make out another voice, one higher pitched, the unmistakable screams of children.

Samuel considered his options, he could not just walk out there and help, that would accomplish nothing, but he could not just leave, there were children in there, and their parents were not making any progress, there just was not enough of them.

Samuel would have to go in there and try to get the kids of himself, chances were that all he would accomplish was getting killed along with them, but if he did not, they would certainly die.

He moved around to the back of the building, as silently as he could, entering a small back garden. Samuel tried to find a way in; Samuel could not see a back door, and all the windows on the ground floor were too small. He looked up to and saw a window on the first floor that just might be big enough.

There was a wooden beam he could use to climb up. He grabbed onto it and began to head upwards, the wood had been smoothed by decades of rain, so there was little risk of splinters, but it made it more challenging. The fire had heated it up so much his skin on his palm was close to blistering, when he reached the first floor, he found struts blocking the window.

"Bugger," said Samuel trying hard to keep his voice hushed. Samuel grabbed one of the struts and pulled. It took some effort, less than he thought, however, the fire had weakened the wood, and after a quick struggle the strut did come away it hit the ground with a thud but no one came to investigate. After a quick tug of war with the rest of the beams, the window was finally clear, and Samuel entered the building.

The heat was tremendous while the smoke stung his eyes and aggravated his lungs. Samuel was in a bedroom, it was quite small with a double bed and a dresser and two chairs. He headed towards the door, it had no door handle or knob so Samuel just pushed against it and it opened.

Samuel had to place his hoodie's sleeve over his mouth and nose to limit the amount of soot he breathed in. He could hear the voices of the children coming from his left, two doors down, at the end of the hallway.

He made his way to the door and paused for a second. Samuel knew what would happen when he opened the door and he did not want to go through all of that again, but if he did not they would die. "Sometimes you just have to do things you don't like Samuel," he told himself and pushed open the door.

Huddled in the corner of a second bedroom were three children a Lamia girl, an insectoid boy and a weresheep girl – the very same trio he had met at the start of all this. Samuel might have called it fate if he believed in such a thing.

The insectoid boy looked at the door and a look of horror Samuel knew all too well rocketed across his face. He wildly patted the other two and pointed at Samuel, the second the weresheep caught sight of him she let out an enormous scream. After she had finished, Samuel was able to hear frantic cries coming from outside. The Lamia, however, acted differently, she just sat there staring at Samuel.

Samuel took four steps forward; the insectoid began to cry while the weresheep hugged the other two even tighter. Samuel got down on one knee and looked the Lamia straight in the eye and said: "I know you're afraid of me, I know you don't trust me, but please believe me I do not want to hurt you I just want to help you." Samuel then extended his right hand to the girl with his palm face up.

The Lamia girl looked at Samuel's hand and then to his face, Samuel trying his hardest to make a kind and approachable face, she looked deeply into his eye while her friend kept muttering to her. Samuel thought he was getting nowhere when suddenly her arm came away from the trembling insectoid boy. It slowly extended to Samuel, who did not move an inch, while the weresheep pleaded with her friend, and placed her hand in his.

Then Samuel heard a sound above him, a slow creaking sound, and looked up. And saw a massive beam heading straight for his skull. Samuel felt something impact against his chest, and he found himself lying on his back several feet from where he had once stood. Samuel regained his composure and was able to see a huge wood beam embedded in the floor and young Lamia coiling her tail back up. "You saved my life," Samuel said to the young snake girl "Thank you."

The girl nodded, even if she could not understand the words she did understand his intent, she then turned around and talked to the other two, grabbed hold of them and pulled them to their feet. The weresheep and insectoid, however, were not so keen to trust Samuel; they kept trying to sit back down again until the Lamia punched them both on the head and began to yell at them.

She shouted and screamed and the two stood bolt upright, and Samuel said with a look of surprise "I guess there is something you fear even more than me." The Lamia then grabbed both their wrists and then dragged the closer to Samuel and gave him a look that seemed to say "we will follow." So Samuel led his party out of the room.

He stepped out of the child's bedroom and took a look to his right and managed to make out a set of stairs three doors down. He gestured to them and turned to face the children the Lamia girl nodded, and they all moved towards them. Samuel was careful where he stood the floor made disheartening creaks with every step. He looked behind himself to see if the children were doing ok. The Lamia was following Samuel's lead, taking extra care about where she placed her weight. The other two, however, had their eyes focused directly on Samuel as though they expected him to eat them at any minute. His eyes meet theirs for just an instant, and Samuel turned his head forward, he hated the way they looked at him.

He stopped at the top of the stairs, the children stopped following too, he placed a tentative foot on the first step it did not give way, so he put his full weight on it. It groaned underfoot, but it did not break. Samuel began to descend the stairs, he gave a quick look behind, the children were still following, and then placed his attention firmly on where he was stepping.

Samuel and the children reached the bottom without incident. He was now in a kitchen; Samuel felt it was odd to have the stairs leading to the first floor to be in a kitchen but "each to their own" he said aloud. The kitchen had a simple stove by a small window on the wall furthest wall and a set of tables and chairs in the centre.

There was an exit to his left and Samuel headed for it. He was in a small hallway, and to his right, he saw the main entrance. From the other side, he could hear the frantic cries of the children's parents, his three companions began to call back and made their way to the door. There was a problem, however, not just the fire, another beam had fallen and was blocking the door so that it could not be opened.

He walked towards the door and moved the children out of the way. The beam lay at an angle, and he believed that he should be able to push it out of the way, at least long enough for the kids to get through. He placed his right shoulder against the wood, put his left foot on the wall, and pushed.

Samuel strained himself, and while the beam moved he could not lift it far enough so that the door could open. He relaxed and let the beam settle again. Taking a step back Samuel tried to think about it, he rubbed his finger and tapped his feet, and then it came to him, he needed more leverage.

He took out his knife and embedded it in the door, Samuel then positioned himself in the same way he had before and pushed the flat of the blade against the beam while his legs worked with it. The beam began to move, and Samuel found that it was much easier than before. The beam kept moving when finally, the door started to open ever so slightly.

A hand appeared from behind the door, it was covered in wool. The weresheep girl rushed to the door and began to hold her mother's hand all the while sobbing and calling out to her. Samuel was suddenly galvanised, and he removed his blade and placed it closer to the wooden beam and pushed again the beam moved further up. Samuel kept doing this, using his knife as a lever, until the gap was finally big enough of the children to squeeze through.

"Go on!" Samuel yelled at the sheep girl making a motion with his head to get her to leave. She was startled slightly by his raised voice, and whether she understood what Samuel meant or she was just wanted to get away, the girl squeezed through the door.

Samuel looked at the insectoid and said: "ok you next!" The boy just stood there too worried that Samuel would try something if he got any closer, "hurry I can't hold it up forever" Samuel shouted. Then the Lamia placed her hand on his shoulder and pushed him towards the door.

The boy made a slow advance never once taking his eyes of Samuel, who in turn never stopped looking at him. When he finally reached the door, he paused for about five seconds and then dashed through the door. Samuel could hear the relived [relieved] cried [cries] of the adults as a second child had managed to escape, but he heard another sound, the sound of creaking metal. Almost without thinking he pulled away from the door just as the blade of the knife shattered and a large chunk of metal embedded itself in his left shoulder.

"AAAGGGGHHH, SHIT!" Samuel screamed into the air. The pain was indescribable, and he lost all strength in his legs. The Lamia rushed to his side and tried to keep him still. Then her attention suddenly focused on the door, and Samuel believed that the door had a gap in it and she was going to leave him here, but suddenly she placed her arms under his and with all of her strength pulled him to the other end of the corridor.

The next thing Samuel heard was a sound like a tree splitting in half, and the entire front portion of the house came crashing down. Dust and ash filled the whole room, and Samuel had to cover his face or else he might have gone blind.

Samuel grabbed the little girl by her waist and dragged her into the kitchen. The dust was much thinner in here.

Before tending to himself, he checked to see if the child was unharmed. She was coated in ash and coughing gently, but she did not appear to have a scratch on her. His quick check-up done, he focus on the wound in his shoulder it was deep, and a steady flow of blood was coming out of it. But he could not leave it in there, so he pulled his sleeve over his right hand and grabbed the broken blade and in a quick motion, he ripped it out of his arm.

Samuel clutched his shoulder and contracted into a foetal position. The Lamia picked herself up and made her way to Samuel's side. She held Samuel's head and looked into his eyes, Samuel looked right back and saw that her eyes were red and watering due to the smoke, the girl spoke to Samuel and tried to pull him to his feet. Samuel was impressed by the girl's determination and not wanting to be outdone by a kid, he dragged himself to his feet.

Samuel looked around for another way out. He walked to the kitchen window but found that the window was far too small for even for the girl to get through. "Come on Samuel think" he yelled at himself "There has to be another way out." Samuel rubbed his finger for comfort; his mind was coming up blank.

Samuel felt something touch his left hand he turned to see that the girl had placed her hand in his and she gave him a looked of supreme confidence. Samuel closed his eyes and began to think. There had to be a way out other than the front door, after all, he had got in. "The top floor window, that how we get out," he said to the girl.

Samuel held her hand tight and led her to the stairs. The fire had progressed rapidly and was even fiercer now. Samuel placed his foot on the step, and it gave a horrendous squeal, they did not have much time. Samuel walked quickly up the stairs when he was halfway up one of the steps gave way, and his right foot fell through. The Lamia held onto his hand even tighter. Samuel was able to pull his foot back through with only a few scrapes to show for it, he and the girl reached the top of the stairs just as the entire staircase came crashing down behind them "we're not going back that way" said Samuel.

The air was becoming unbreathable they had to get out of there now; Samuel headed straight for the nearest room, as he pushed open the door a large gust of air rushed past him, and the flames became even stronger, Samuel pushed the girl into the bedroom and slammed the door shut behind them.

Walking to the same window he had entered he looked down. It was a four-metre drop to the ground "I can survive that" Samuel said to himself. The roof began to creak, and Samuel knew it would not last much longer. They had to leave now, but the window was not large enough for both of them to jump out side by side.

He took in a deep breath of the horrid air and scooped the girl up in his arms, and the child was quite startled by this. She was rather heavy, and her tail was making it awkward, but the Lamia apparently sensed this, and she began to wrap her tail around his waist. Samuel's shoulder was in incredible pain as the girl's weight forced his injury open. He shuffled onto the window sill. Samuel's fear of heights came back to him in all its fury, but Samuel did not let that stop him for even a second, and he jumped out of the window.

As Samuel fell he tried to land on both of his feet to spread the weight of both him and the girl, but her tail pulled him down to his right. As his right leg hit the ground, Samuel heard and felt a sickening crunch followed by tremendous pain. He had broken his leg.

The rest of his body hit the ground with a thud, and the girl landed on top of him winding him in the process. Samuel screamed and swore into the night and then, rather harshly, shoved the girl off him. The girl toppled away from him and lay in a slight clump, for a moment Samuel was afraid that he had hurt her, but after a brief moment of motionlessness she got up as though nothing had happened.

Samuel held his leg loosely, the pain in his shoulder wholly overcome, and his eyes became teary, but Samuel could not stay here, his pained cried would bring people to him and in his weakened state he could not defend himself. Samuel crawled to his feet and started to hobble away.

Samuel could hear frenzied but relieved voices behind him. Samuel did not look behind him, he could not afford the time, and to be honest, he expected an arrow or knife in the back, but nothing happened at all. Samuel's painful walk remained undisturbed; he made his way to the forest. His breathing became heavy, he cried and more than once he fell to the ground.

It took him until dawn to reach home, in that time he met no one, no angry dogs or pitchfork-wielding villagers. He walked down the steps, replacing the slab before making his way to the cavern. Samuel sat down on the floor resting his back on the stone when fatigue and pain took him, and he was asleep.

Epilogue

Several days past [passed], Samuel had tied a piece of wood to his leg in a makeshift splint and was using a large stick as a crutch. Samuel believed that the fall had split the bone right down the middle. The injury in his shoulder still hurt but had healed quickly and was only a dull ache now.

Samuel rested on a ledge, he had, had a reprieve from the hallucinations and depression in his time since his rescue of the children, but it had all started to come back. Samuel was just emotionally tired.

Samuel had his eyes closed trying to keep his mind focused when he heard something, a distant sound, calling out to him. He heard things again; Samuel rubbed his finger and tried to ignore it. However, something was different about it this time; the sound was actually come from somewhere.

Propping himself up on his crutch Samuel tried to locate the source but the cavern was making it echo. Samuel moved around, and the sound suddenly stopped, he assumed that he had just imagined it, but as he passed the entrance the noise began again. He could hear it more clearly this time, it was coming from the dry room, it was coming from outside.

"So they found me," said Samuel. His first thought was to escape through the tunnel, the one he had used the first time he had entered the cavern. "Nah" Samuel sighed he could not swim with this leg; no he would face them and whatever they intended to do head on.

Samuel headed down the dry room, every time his stick hit the floor a loud clack echoed all around, it took him three times longer than usual to make it to the end. The shouting would stop for a while and then start all over again. When he finally reached the steps, he moved the slab out of the way and hopped his way up.

Samuel expected to see an angry mob but what he actually saw was a blond haired Lamia. Samuel climbed up the last few steps and limped, out of the extension, over to her.

The girl stood her ground and just looked directly at Samuel. He noticed something different in her face this time, there was no fear he could detect or wariness, she looked at Samuel as though he was a person.

"Hey kid," said Samuel "what are you doing here?" Samuel looked to his left and then his right looking for anyone else but saw no one. "Just you?" He added. The girl just smiled back at him. Her eyes moved to Samuel's shoulder and leg, she then turned to look at his face once again. "It's alright I'll live," said Samuel with a slight nod trying to reassure her "thank you for caring" he added. Samuel realised that she had her hands behind her back "what have you got there?" Samuel asked pointing behind her. She smiled again and revealed what she had been hiding. It was a knife, it had an ornate handle with a leather scabbard. She held it up in both hands and presented it to Samuel.

"For me?" Samuel asked, pointing to himself, and he stretched out his left hand and picked it up. Samuel removed it from its holder and examined the blade; it was incredibly sharp and shined in the sun.

Samuel held it firmly and gave it a little swing, after examining it thoroughly he put it back and said: "thank you, it's very thoughtful of you, but I don't have anything for you." Samuel's arms relaxed, his hands brushed past his pocket, and he felt something, a figurine he had carved a few weeks ago.

He rummaged around in his pocket there it was, he removed the crude Lamia statue from his pocket, he had utterly forgotten about it even though he had been carrying around all of this time. Samuel rotated it in his hands and presented it to the girl "it's not much, but I hope you like it."

The girl looked at the figure and reached out to take it. The girl picked it up and examined it from every angle when suddenly she giggled and her face positively beaming she said something to Samuel, and even though he did not understand the words, he knew what she had said. For the first time since he came to this place Samuel smiled, he genuinely smiled, and Samuel said: "Well maybe it isn't so bad here after all."

Glossary

Chitin - A material that an insect's exoskeleton is made from.

Insectoid - Possessing the qualities of an insect.

Lamia - A Greek woman cursed by the Gods, typically portrayed as a woman with a snake's tail for legs.

Effigy - A figurine or statue in the image or likeness of a person.

Napalm - A highly combustible chemical weapon, its most infamous use was during the Vietnam war.

Printed in Great Britain
by Amazon